HEARTS
to Mend

CHRISTINA BERRY

For Meghan,
the stroke coordinator to my heart.

And Dr. Thomas McMinn,
thank you for mending the hole in my heart.

NOTE FROM THE AUTHOR

In general, *Hearts to Mend* is a lighthearted love story with several sexy bits. However, some scenes might be upsetting to some readers. This book contains detailed descriptions of a fire emergency and a major medical crisis, as well as mentions of alcoholism, drug abuse, elder and child neglect, and animal suffering.

There's cussing and fucking, too.

Enjoy!
Christina

"When you gonna propose, Catman?" Rooster crows at Drew as he scrubs the grill of Engine 31.

It's our weekly Big Truck shift at the fire station, when we clean and maintain the apparatus. This week we're getting the truck extra clean for the local first graders, who are taking a tour of the firehouse tomorrow. And Rooster, being Rooster, likes to liven up our long shifts by nagging Drew.

Drew rolls his eyes as he grumbles, "Dude, let me finish building the house before you sign me up for a new project."

"Marriage isn't a project, *dude*. It's a privilege and a lifelong commitment. Maybe it's the *commitment* that's got you running scared." Rooster pokes the bear, and I have to bite my lips together to keep from cackling.

"I'm not running anywhere." Drew sounds like he's complaining, but he's got a dumb grin on his pretty-boy face.

Our Catman is a smitten kitten for Chloe. But who wouldn't be? She's a sweetheart and gorgeous. Drew was a goner from day one. Then her house burned down—with her and their cats still in it—and

Drew's priorities got real clear real fast. Priority numero uno: Chloe. Now they're building a new house on the land where Chloe's family farm once stood.

Drew continues defending himself. "I'm not afraid of commitment, not with Chloe. But a *wedding* is a huge project. I need to pace myself."

I take the bait he's reeled out for us. "I heard Al at the hardware store has eyes for your girl. Be careful you don't wait too long—he might swoop in and steal her heart."

Drew shakes his head and laughs as he scrubs the windshield. "Al is eighty-two years old. And he's deeply in love with Inez Rodriguez."

"All's we're saying is—"

Right on cue, Rooster hits the sound on his phone, and the little speaker we brought in this morning starts blasting Beyonce's classic *Single Ladies.* The two of us jump off the rig and sync right into a flawless execution of the dance from the video—or as flawless as two firefighters with four left feet and only a week of practice can muster.

A few of the neighborhood dog walkers stop to watch the show as we squat, twist, and shimmy on the driveway in front of the firehouse.

Watts comes out of the station carrying the agenda for our shift and frowns, but only for a moment before he starts doing the wrist flip put-a-ring-on-it move with us.

Drew howls with laughter as he hoses the hood of the engine then turns the water on us. Only Watts manages to escape without getting sprayed.

As we shake off the water, Watts, easily able to guess the reason for our song choice, offers his own bit of wisdom to Drew. "Don't let these two pressure you. Don't pop that question until you know it's right."

"For fuck's sake, I know it's right. Chloe is it for me, but can you all just wait for me to finish building her damn dream house before you have me making every other major life move?"

"Sure, we can lay off." I relent... Sort of. The guy is like my kid brother. I can't help but smother him with big-sister advice. "But, Drew, life doesn't come at you in order. You don't get everything in a nice, neat to-do list with items you can check off one by one. Don't put off important shit because you have other important shit to do."

"Wise woman." Watts points at me. "Listen to Dee, Catman. She gets it."

Thinking of my own love life—or rather the lack thereof—doesn't make me feel so wise. In my adult life, I've missed every cue, every opportunity, every major life event, still stuck nursing a broken heart. I'd wanted to get married, right in the middle of everything, but the love of my life said no. He wanted "to live a little" first. He wanted to take things in order. So instead of marrying me, he went off to war and broke my heart from half a world away.

Watts bestows his fatherly advice to Drew. "You know, my daughter came just six months after our wedding, just three months after we bought the house. Everything hit at once for us, and it was a lot to handle, but I wouldn't change a thing."

My heart squeezes at the thought of Watts's lovely family. If I had his life, I wouldn't change a thing either. But a lovely family life isn't in the cards for me, apparently, and there's no use dwelling, right?

I tuck all those memories and icky feelings away—not in the mood for them today. The sun is shining, the breeze is blowing, the truck is sparkling, and life is good. I'm a badass woman with a killer bod and the wit to match. While I doubt I'll ever find a storybook love like I used to know, there are plenty of other kinds of happiness.

Doris the dispatcher's voice comes over the loudspeaker in the station. "Engine 31 and Medic 12, respond to injured child, Navarro Elementary School playground."

Well, that's certainly not happiness. But it has us moving. We grab our gear, jump in the engine, and race to the school.

Navarro Elementary School is close to the station. But that's not saying much. Everything is close to everything in a town the size of Krause. It takes us under five minutes to arrive on scene.

The playground, normally a cacophony of happy children, is eerily quiet now. In hushed voices, teachers try to corral curious children, but they're ignored. Everyone's attention is riveted to the monkey bars at the center of the playground, where Anne Griffin, one of the first-grade teachers, sits cross-legged on the ground cradling a little boy in her arms.

Rooster slings the medic bag over his shoulder, and we cross the fine gravel of the playground to the center of the scene. I take the lead on this call, pulling on my latex gloves as I get down on my knees in front of Anne, trying to block the view of all those little lookie-loos hovering around.

My assessing gaze moves over the boy in her arms. He looks so small, enveloped in his teacher's embrace with his little legs dangling out over her knee. His face is pinched tight with pain, his eyes screwed shut, his olive complexion sallow. He hugs his injured arm against his chest as Anne rocks him gently in her lap.

"Well, hi there," I say to the boy. "What happened?"

He answers in a small voice. "I fell."

"It's his wrist. I think it's broken." Anne rubs his back gently.

"Ouch," I say to the boy, always addressing him directly. When I was a kid, I hated how the grown-ups would talk *about* me and never *to* me, so I'm careful not to make that mistake with the kids I work with. "You must be pretty tough. When I broke my wrist, I cried and cried. It hurt something fierce! Does yours hurt?"

He nods stiffly.

"What's your name?"

With a little sniffle, he answers, "Mateo."

"Well, hi, Mateo. I'm Dee, and these are my friends Drew, Watts, and Rooster." Mateo peeks one eye open, looking at the men who stand behind me and block the view of all those prying eyes. The boy stares at the guys intently, probably wondering which one is named Rooster. Acting like it's a secret, I cup my mouth and tell him, "We call him that because of his red hair."

Just for a moment, I get the hint of a smile from Mateo, and I smile back at him. "Can I see where it hurts?"

Mateo screws his eyes shut again and clamps his jaw tight, trying so hard not to cry as he loosens his grip on his injured arm so I can look. It's swollen and discolored, and I'd guess the same diagnosis as Anne: likely broken. "Ouch. That must hurt."

He nods again.

"You know, Mateo, it's okay to cry. Even the toughest big strong men cry sometimes because they know that when you have hurt feelings locked inside you, you need to get them out. So you can put those feelings in your tears and let them go. Then, maybe it won't hurt as much inside anymore. Okay?"

Mateo frowns, but he blinks up at me. He has the sweetest brown eyes, glistening with tears. One escapes and trickles down his cheek. My heart cracks wide open for the kid.

I turn to my team. "ETA on EMS?"

"Thirty minutes. They have a patient transfer," Watts states quietly. I trade a look with him, and he nods, already knowing what I'm thinking.

Turning back to Mateo, I give him a sideways smile. "Mateo, would you like to ride in a fire engine?"

His little eyes light up, as if his pain is forgotten, and he starts squirming out of Anne's lap like he's going to hop up, right as rain. Rooster and Drew quickly come down on their knees on either side of me, encouraging him to remain seated long enough to get a splint on his arm, immobilizing it for transport to the hospital.

It's not every day we transport a patient in our engine. It's not exactly protocol, but Mateo is hurting, and the hospital is two minutes away. No need to keep him waiting here. Plus, Mateo's been such a good patient, I want to turn this experience into a memory he'll cherish, at least in part.

So up and at 'em we go. Watts is already back at the engine, calling ahead to cancel the ambulance and prepare the hospital for our arrival. Mateo walks himself to the truck, flanked by Drew and Rooster, making sure he doesn't fall and further injure his arm.

I hang back with Anne and Mrs. Strahan, who's been the school principal since back in my day. In a whisper, Mrs. Strahan informs me, "We've left several messages with Mateo's father, but he's not answering his phone. I'm going to try his grandmother when I get back to my office. Anne, you should accompany him to the hospital with his parental release forms so he's not alone."

"I'll stay with him." I volunteer before I've truly thought it through. But it's a slow day, and my shift ends in half an hour anyway. So yeah, I'll stay with Mateo until a member of his family shows up at the hospital.

The teachers glance at each other, silently conferring among themselves, then provide me with a copy of Mateo's emergency medical release paperwork, giving me quick hugs before I hustle to catch up with my team as they put away the gear.

I step up into the crew cab to find Drew and Rooster have strapped Mateo into one of the jump seats between them. And Drew is fitting an intercom headset over Mateo's ears so he can listen to our chatter.

I give the kid a thumbs-up, which he returns with his good hand, and when we're all strapped in and ready to go, I blast the siren to impress his schoolyard friends. Mateo squeals with joy.

"Prepare for popularity, Mateo. Everyone's going to want to sign your cast tomorrow," Rooster says.

"I get a cast?" Mateo asks, his voice filled with excitement that echoes over the radio.

A couple of the guys chuckle.

I shake my head. *Little boys are so weird.*

CHAPTER 2
RICO

"Did the school finally reach you?"

"The school?" I blink at Gloria, the *Krause Gazette* receptionist for the last fifteen years.

She looks frazzled, as usual, with two different colored pins sticking out of a messy bun on the top of her head. "About Mateo's accident."

"Mateo had an accident?" Now *I'm* frazzled. My blood runs cold, my heart plummets to my feet, and my head spins with panic.

Fumbling for the phone in my pocket, I remember the requirement to put it on silent during the new-employee orientation session with human resources. Getting it out, I glance at the screen, and my panic worsens.

Eight missed calls. *Fuck.*

I listen to the first message, time-stamped from almost an hour ago. "Hello, this message is for Ricardo Rodriguez. This is Principal Delores Strahan calling from Navarro Elementary School. At recess today, Mateo fell on the playground, and we fear he may have broken his arm. We've called 911, and they are—"

"Fuck. Fuck. Fuck!"

Gloria frowns at me, but I don't have time to concern myself with her delicate sensibilities. In a matter of seconds, I'm out the front door and across the blacktop, practically sliding over the hood of my Charger like I'm in an episode of *The Dukes of Hazzard*. Once I'm in, engine revved, I gun it out of the lot toward the hospital.

I can't believe I didn't check my phone. What kind of shitty father doesn't regularly check his phone? My boy needed me. He's hurting and alone, and I've neglected him. Jesus, I'm no better than his mom.

Parking quickly at the hospital, I jog inside to address the woman at the front desk. "My son came in from the elementary school. His name is Mateo Rodriguez—"

"Oh, yes, such a little sweetheart and cute as a button," the woman says.

I wait for her to say more, trying to remind myself this isn't the city —every conversation takes a little bit longer here—but when she still doesn't tell me where to find Mateo, I ask, "Can I see him?"

"Sure. Just need to see some ID."

I hand over my license, bouncing impatiently from foot to foot as she inspects my identity. Finally, she calls over a nurse to escort me to Matty's room.

Matty startles, mid-laughter, as I burst through the door and come at him, touching every inch of his head and shoulders, checking for injuries behind his ears. He doesn't seem to have a scratch on him except for the red plaster cast coating his left arm from knuckles to elbow.

"I just got the message that you were hurt. I'm so sorry I wasn't here sooner, big guy. Are you okay?"

Matty lets me smother him in a hug, but eventually he wiggles free and points across the room. "I'm okay, Daddy. Dee kept me company. She's funny."

I nod—glad he wasn't alone—then stop. Everything stops. Inside me, my heart, my lungs, my brain… It all stops. Did he say Dee? As in *my* Dee?

Someone clears their throat, and before I can fully process my thoughts, I hear her voice for the first time in eight years. "Well, kiddo, now that your dad is here, I'll get going. You take care, buddy."

That voice. God, I've missed her voice.

There were times when the sound of her voice—soft, sweet, and a little raspy—was the only thing that could soothe me. Of course, there were other times when she could cut me to the quick with a single word.

I've missed it all, both her soft words and her sharp ones. I've missed everything about her, from her laughter to the way she butchered Spanish to the sound of her sighs when I touched her just right. I miss the taste of her—

"Bye, Dee, I'll see you tomorrow." My son waves at the person behind me, and only then do I muster the courage to turn and look.

There, standing in front of the chair in the corner of the room— which I'd passed without notice on my way to Matty's bedside—is the first woman I ever loved. By most measures, the *only* woman I've ever loved.

All the air rushes out of my lungs as I take in the sight of her. Dee was hot in high school, with long blond hair, gorgeous green eyes, and legs for days. But now, all grown up, she takes my breath away. Even in her work pants and fire department T-shirt, she's stunning.

I stand there staring at her like an idiot. I should probably say something, but what?

When I moved back home, I knew I'd run into her—it's a small town. But I wasn't expecting it to be here. Now. With my son present and beaming at her like she's the tooth fairy.

Dee looks surprised. I guess the rumor mill hadn't informed her of my return. Her eyes scan over me from head to toe and back again, and for a moment, just one tiny little second, she looks happy to see me. Then her expression falls. The beautiful smile directed at my son slips, and her eyes turn cold, guarded, like she's built a wall between us.

"Hi, Rico. It's been a while."

She steps closer. Close enough that I can smell the honeysuckle sweetness of her shampoo. It's the same scent I remember, and it sends a jolt of electricity straight to my heart. But she looks away from me, past me, to my son. They do some elaborate handshake with Matty's good hand, then she squeezes his shoulder before she turns to leave.

Matty and I watch her go, like we both wish she would stay, and before I can think better of it, I turn to my son and ask him, "Will you give me a sec, big man? I need to talk to Dee for a moment."

With a nod from Matty, I move out into the hall looking for Dee. She's easy to spot, moving fast toward the exit in a shirt with FIRE written across the back in bright yellow letters.

"Dee Dee," I holler as I jog to catch up.

She freezes at the sound of that old nickname and spins to face me, frowning. "Look, I didn't know he was your son. Okay?"

"Huh?"

"Jesus. I didn't plan this. If that's what you're thinking."

"No, I..." *What?* "I just wanted to thank you for being here for Matty."

"It's my job."

I don't know what I expected my reunion with Dee to be like, but this isn't it. She's angry—I expected that. But it's obvious—probably more obvious than she'd like it to be—that she's hurting too. It's like the pain I caused her all those years ago is still fresh and sharp and right beneath the surface.

She does that thing she used to always do when she was upset: press her lips together and pick at the freckle on her chin. It's strangely endearing that she hasn't changed that little habit.

After a moment, she asks, "So you live here now?"

I nod, and it feels like too much, like a bobblehead nod. "Living with Mom at the moment, moving into the rental next door once Mom's tenants move out."

"Drew and Chloe."

"Huh?"

"Inez's tenants are Drew and Chloe. You're back in a small town. You can call people by their actual names here."

I blink, a little lost.

"Well, bye," Dee says and starts to turn away, but I don't want her to go.

Even if all she's giving me is her anger, I'll take it. I'll take anything from her for another moment to stare into those sea-glass green eyes and revel in all the memories elicited by the smell of her hair. Desperate to stop her from leaving, I step closer and almost reach for her as I say, "Dee—"

"What, Rico?" She raises her voice, and there's fire in her eyes when she says, "What do you have to say to me that's more important than being with your son right now?"

Ouch. The censure cuts deep. And in my head, I hear the word "neglect" on repeat. I take a step back, moving farther from Dee and closer to my son.

"And next time, answer your phone" are her parting words as she turns away, her long legs taking her out the door and out of my life again.

I go back to Matty's room, practicing my smile as I push the door open. Despite my best efforts, Matty knows how to read my expression, and he blinks those owl eyes at me. "What's wrong, Daddy?"

"Well, my favorite son got hurt today." I sit on the edge of his bed. "That's pretty wrong."

"I'm your only son," he insists with a giggle.

"You are?" I scrunch up my face like I'm doing the math in my head, then ask, "Well, how is my only favorite son feeling?"

"I'm okay now." He gets serious when he adds, "I cried and got the hurt feelings out."

"Oh? That's good."

"Do you cry, Daddy?"

"Sometimes." *Never.*

"Dee says that when you cry you can put your hurt feelings in the tears and let them out."

"Well, that's pretty smart of her." I ruffle his hair as I swallow all the feelings welling up at the thought of Dee espousing wisdom to my boy, then work up something to say. "I'm going to put my feelings into words and let them out that way. Do you want to hear them?"

He nods.

"My feelings are that I love you very much, and I'm ready to get you home for some yummy dinner and a lot of rest tonight. You've got a big day tomorrow."

His eyes light up with excitement. "I got to ride in the fire truck today, and Dee says she'll show me how to make the siren go really loud tomorrow when we tour the station."

I cringe. I'd been referring to his first day back to school with a cast, remembering how popular my cast made me when I broke my arm in third grade. It was the week I caught Dee's attention. But Matty's mention of the field trip to the fire station reminds me: I signed up to be a chaperone. Apparently, I signed up as a chaperone for a tour of *Dee's* firehouse, before I even knew she was a firefighter.

"Are you sure you want to be into men?" I grumble between gulps of my beer. "Men are awful."

Rooster chuckles. "Can't help it. I love cock."

With a harrumph, I commiserate: "Same." Then I laugh, a little drunk. "Ha! Rooster loves cock!"

Rooster raises a brow at me and tips his beer toward mine as I take another gulp. "That is your final beer, doll, so make it last."

"He has a child!" I shout at the ceiling of Rooster's den, again.

"Yep."

"He told me he loved me, over and over, and he just needed some time to 'live a little.' Then he went off to war and came home with a *child!*"

"Sorry, doll. What can I say? Love hurts."

"You knew didn't you?"

"Dee, everyone knows."

"Well, how come I didn't know?"

"Because the people of this town learned long ago not to talk to you about Rico. You were angry and hurt over the breakup, and no one wanted to rub salt in that wound."

"The breakup? It wasn't a breakup. It was a letter. It was a letter home from Afghanistan telling me not to wait for him. And that was seven years ago. No one thought it might be a good idea to warn me that Rico is not only back home from the war, but also a fucking father?"

Rooster looks at me with empathy in his eyes. I've answered my own question. No one wanted to be the one to inform me for precisely this reason. I'm a wet rag, draped across Rooster's couch, cussing to the heavens between sips of his favorite lager. Who was going to volunteer for tell-Dee-about-Rico duty? No sane person, that's for sure.

"He was supposed to have kids *with* me." *Sorry Rooster, but I need to vent.* "He said I was the one, so how could he walk away from the person he supposedly loved?"

Rooster grimaces. "He didn't walk away. He joined the Army."

"And then he walked away."

Rooster eyes me as he takes a sip of his beer.

"What? Why are you looking at me like that?"

"I think you need to talk to him."

"About what?"

"About why he left. About what happened. You need to hear his side."

Fuck that noise. I'm not giving Rico one more second of my time, my patience, or my understanding. He broke my heart and started a life with another woman, had a *child*. He deserves nothing from me.

But I have so many questions. Why did he join the Army when he could have found work here? Why did he write me that break-up letter? Was it because he'd met her, this mysterious mother of Mateo? And where is she? Why didn't Matty's mom turn up at the hospital? Not to mention: Why is Rico back in town? Why had he never reached out? And why, after all these years, did seeing him again send my heart into hysterics? Why do I still feel anything for him other than rage? Why can't I ever stop thinking about him?

"I should go," I mumble.

"Oh no you don't, you beautiful dummy. You're sleeping in the guest room tonight. I've already hidden your car keys."

"What? I've only had two beers."

"And nothing to eat. You're mad and semi-drunk, and I will not be letting you on the road until morning. No use arguing. The sheets are clean. Go to bed."

I stare at him a moment, then stick my tongue out.

"I love you too, doll. Now off you go. We have to be presentable for the kiddos tomorrow. No hangovers allowed."

Grumbling, I drag myself off the couch to stand. Rooster stands, too, so he can wrap his insanely long arms around me in the softest hug. I squeeze my arms around his waist, bury my face in the warmth of his chest, and let myself fall apart, just for a moment.

He strokes my hair as I silently cry, shaking more than sobbing. I was never much of a crier, but when my mood sinks this low, I let it out. Rooster has been my shoulder to cry on more times than I can count. Before Rooster, it was Rico. As far back as I can remember, it was always Rico.

My first best friend. My first love. My *only* love. Rico was it for me, from the time we were eight years old, riding dirt bikes and catching crawdads in the creek. Rico wasn't just my best friend, he was my only friend. He was the only person I ever needed. When my parents fought and pills stole my mom while alcohol numbed my dad, I was never alone because I had Rico.

Then he left.

I should have seen it coming. While I was dreaming of a happily-ever-after future with him, he was talking to the Army recruiter. While I saw only him in my future, he saw a big, wide world he wanted to conquer first.

Rico hadn't been ready to settle down with me, settle *for* me. So he left, and he broke my heart beyond repair. But now he's back. And he looks so good. He's been handsome since the day he was born, but the sight of him in navy slacks and a button-down shirt rolled up at the sleeves sent my heart into a fluttery tizzy.

He's grown into his long, lanky height too. The Army filled him out, made him strong, with broad shoulders and thick forearms laced with veins that bulged when he squeezed his hands at his sides.

At the time, I wondered why he did that. Was it to stop himself from reaching for me? And damn my stupid heart—I'd wanted him to reach for me so badly. Despite everything, despite all the reasonable voices in my head telling me to run far away from that heartbreaker, all I really wanted was to feel his arms around me, breathe his scent into my lungs, and drown in him completely.

Pathetic. I'm a glutton for pain and punishment. Why not let him tie me to a post and flog me? It would probably hurt less than this. And I'd probably whine a lot less about it too.

Deidre Marie Fletcher—I can practically hear my mom's voice in my head—*men aren't worth all this bellyachin'. You want love and devotion? Get a dog.*

Gently pulling away from Rooster, I flash him an anemic smile as I wipe my eyes dry. "Thanks."

"For what? The beer?"

"For always being there for me."

Rooster grins from one corner of his mouth and rubs his knuckles over my hair, like a big brother. I love him for it. I don't feel quite as alone in this world when Rooster treats me like a bratty kid sister.

With a kiss to his cheek, I turn and aim for his guest bedroom, kicking off my boots before collapsing into bed. I'm exhausted, worse than the exhaustion I usually feel after a shift. Thankfully, all I have to do tomorrow is host two dozen six-year-olds as they run roughshod all over the station.

CHAPTER 4
RICO

"Sorry about the incident yesterday." I glance up at my editor, Dan, who is standing at the corner of my desk, looking contrite and shaggy. The shaggy look is a constant—his tie permanently askew—but the contrition is new. "I want you to know you're always welcome to keep your phone on in here. In fact, I encourage it."

Oh, right. That.

He continues, "Sandra created the phones-off-during-meetings policy because we had this bleeping intern who never put her bleeping phone down."

Dan has an impressionable four-year-old daughter and a swear jar at home, so he tends to *bleep* his way through conversations. I can empathize. Matty's mind soaks up every word I say like a sponge, and he repeats it all. I'm still trying to get him to unlearn some of the language he heard from his mother.

"But of course, as a reporter, and a dad, you need your phone on. So consider this conversation your official exemption from the phones-off-during-meetings policy."

I smile at the guy. He's the nicest editor I've worked with so far.

The editor of the paper I wrote for in the Army was a jackass, and the one at the weekly in San Antonio was a high-strung mess. Dan has a quiet demeanor, and he trusts his staff to be professional and get their jobs done without a lot of micromanaging. It's a nice change of pace. "Thanks, Dan."

"So, how is Matty?" he leans a hip against my desk, genuinely curious.

"You know kids—they have more resilience than we do. This morning, he couldn't wait to get to school to show all his classmates his cast. And he was bouncing off the walls with excitement about their trip to the firehouse this afternoon. Apparently, Dee promised him he could play with the siren today." I grimace at my casual mention of Dee. Since moving back, a lot of people have asked me if I've seen her, spoken to her. I've deflected as much as I can. But now that I've seen her, spoken to her, she's on my mind constantly.

Dan says, "Speaking of… Rumor has it there were some fireworks at the hospital yesterday."

I groan as I shake my head. "The gossip mill in this town is second to none."

"Well, I am the editor of the bleeping paper. People think I need to know the things that go on around here."

"This isn't going into the paper, is it?"

"Of course not! This isn't some bleeping gossip rag."

"Right."

"Still, I heard it was an interesting reunion." Dan waggles his brows. This might not be a gossip rag, but Dan is still a gossip hound. Everyone here is.

"She's not too happy to see me." *Understatement.* She'd looked at me yesterday like she wanted to flay me alive.

Dan rolls his eyes. "If that's what you think, then you aren't paying attention. Better work on that. I need a reporter who can read people."

I blink at him, a little stunned. But before I can truly comprehend what he's said, he's on to a new subject. "You're out this afternoon, right?"

"Right. Accompanying Matty's class on a field trip."

"To the fire station?"

I nod.

He laughs. "Enjoy."

Wrangling twenty-five first graders is no easy feat. Teachers deserve a lot more credit than they get…and better pay. I'm already exhausted, and we're still on the bus, driving the few miles that separate the school from the fire station. Matty sits a couple of rows behind me, regaling his classmates with tales of riding in the fire engine they're about to see.

And to think I was nervous about him making friends at his new school. I should have known better; Matty could charm the scales off a snake. His teachers have already pulled me aside to tell me how delightful he is and how well he's doing in his classes.

Perhaps the mess with his mom hasn't harmed him as much as I feared. Or if it has, then this move back home was the right decision. I'd hoped a little quality time with his abuela would help him focus, keep him on the straight and narrow. After all, Mom raised three sons and my brothers both turned out relatively well-adjusted. *The jury's still out on me.*

But beyond the positive influence of his amazing grandma, this community is what Matty needed too. The comfort, kindness, and kinship of a small town is a relief after so much time lost in the maze of the big city, the courts, the system.

With a squeal of the bus's air brakes, we come to a stop at the curb in front of the fire station. Matty's teacher, Miss Anne, stands. With great flourish in her voice, she instructs, "All right, children, it's time to play the quiet game as we get off the bus. Let's all zip our lips."

She pantomimes closing a zipper on her mouth in an exaggerated gesture. All the kids on the bus mimic her like little ducklings and fall silent.

Damn. I need to remember that trick on noisy nights at home.

Miss Anne leans over to address me. "Mr. Rodriguez, do you mind bringing up the rear and checking the bus for anything left behind?"

"Absolutely." I take my orders seriously, standing at full attention and turning to face the kids.

I'm a big guy—the Army added a lot of muscle to my 6'3" frame—so I tend to intimidate. I try to soften my expression with a smile for the kids as I count heads. Twenty-five, same number that got on the bus. No one is hiding behind the seats.

As the teachers and a couple of the parents start a follow-the-leader line off the bus, I hang back, winking at Matty as he passes me with a few new friends in tow, then double-check that no one and nothing has been left on the bus. Once I'm out on the lawn of the firehouse, I do another head count and hang back to keep one eye on the perimeter, ensuring all the kids stay within it. And the other eye, I keep on *her*.

Dee steps out from one of the open bay doors and stops beside a shiny red fire engine parked out front. She shines, too, her blond hair sparkling like spun gold in the rays of the sun, as she welcomes the children to her station.

Even in her cargo pants and fire department T-shirt, she's so sexy, those tactical trousers pulling tight across the curve of her fine ass as she bends to hug my son. Guess this settles it—I'm a sucker for a woman in uniform.

Dee is amazing with the kids. She speaks in animated tones, telling hilariously silly stories and truly engaging with the children. She'd make an amazing mom—

When did that become such an attractive quality? Jesus, stop staring at her.

It's an effort to look at anything other than Dee, but the last time I got to sit back and watch her, we were barely more than kids ourselves. She was beautiful then. She's gorgeous now. And she carries herself with such confidence, like she's completely comfortable in her skin.

Not for the first time, I wonder if she's seeing someone. There's no ring on her finger, and no one has said anything to me about a man in Dee's life, but that's not saying much, considering how little anyone has said to me about Dee at all since I returned to town.

You're still staring at her. Pay attention to the kids!

I peel my gaze away from Dee and do another head count. Everyone is present and accounted for, perimeter secure, the sun warm and shining off everything it touches on this fine spring afternoon.

"At ease, soldier," a deep rumbling voice says from my side. I look over to find Drew standing beside me in his FIRE shirt, mimicking my military stance. "So, Rico, Mateo asked me if he can come over and play with the cats tonight. Figured I'd check with Dad before I told him yes."

I blink at the guy, still amused by the obstacle course he built for his three-legged cat in the house he's renting from my mom—the house Matty and I will move into once Drew and Chloe finish building their home on the other side of Mom's place. I bet Matty will want to keep the cat jungle gym and fill the house with cats too. "Sure. We can come over—"

"No need for you to come... I mean—if you have other plans— Chloe and I would love to have dinner with Mateo, and he can watch movies and play with Bodhi and Utah, so you could have a night to yourself. If you wanted. Maybe meet up with an old friend."

Drew turns to watch Dee as she explains why the redheaded man beside her needs to wear his coat and helmet to a fire.

Wait...

What did Drew say about going out? I glance at him, then over at Dee. Is this some kind of matchmaking thing? I'm sure Dee wouldn't appreciate one of her fire brothers playing Cupid, but I love the opportunity he's handed me.

I gladly accept his offer. "That would be great. Mom has church tonight, so yeah, thanks."

"You're welcome. And you're welcome to head up there and join the rest of the group. I can keep an eye on everyone from here."

With a gracious nod, I ascend the lawn to the firehouse drive and stand along with all the kids beneath the boughs of the live oak trees, listening to Dee explain the air mask and tank her colleague is donning.

Once she finishes explaining the apparatus and equipment, another firefighter leads the kids inside for a tour of the station. I hang back, smiling at Matty when he spares me a grin before he high-fives Dee with his good hand and hurries to catch up to his friends.

"You've made a new friend for life," I say.

"Mateo? He's a sweetie."

I smile, still so bewildered by how I helped create such an amazing little person.

Dee watches me a moment, maybe bewildered by the same thing, then turns away to pack items back into the compartments on the truck.

To her back, I ask quietly, "Can we talk?"

She keeps working as she throws out an answer. "I'm a bit busy at the moment."

"Later." I take a deep breath and let it out before mustering the nerve to ask, "Can I cook you dinner tonight?"

She latches one of the compartment doors closed, then turns to me, frowning. But she doesn't say no.

I press. "Matty has a babysitter, and Mom will be at church, so we could talk… About everything that happened."

"*Everything that happened?* My, what a passive way to phrase it."

Shit. She's right. Describing what I did as a thing "that happened" absolves me of responsibility. And if I'm going to explain myself to her, I will have to accept full responsibility for my stupid actions, starting now. "I'd like to talk about what I did, the mistakes I made. I owe you an explanation, at least."

Dee seems surprised by my ownership of my stupidity. She worries her bottom lip between her teeth as she picks at that freckle on her chin again. I learned long ago not to interrupt her when she's "deep thinking," as she used to call it. So I wait.

After a moment, she finally answers, "I'll think about it." Then she walks away.

Confused, I watch her go, my mouth hanging open like I want to say more, press her further. But how?

As she's about to disappear inside the shadows of the station, she spins on her heels. "Go ahead and cook dinner for two. Maybe I'll see you at eight, maybe I won't."

With that, she spins back around, swaying her ass so sweetly as she disappears inside the station.

Well…hot damn! I have a date at eight.

Because, if there's one thing I know about Dee, it's that she's way too curious not to show up.

CHAPTER 5
DEE

I told him eight, but I arrive at seven thirty. It's a lame little power play, but it's all I've got. I'd considered my other option—not showing up at all—but I have too many questions for that.

Damn my curious nature. This Nancy Drew need for answers has always been my downfall. I can never leave well enough alone, always gotta know the who, what, when, where, and why of it all. In a horror movie, I'd die first, the idiot who goes down into the basement to investigate a creepy noise.

So here I stand on Inez Rodriguez's porch. Surprise and a succulent cloud of spicy scents wash over me when she swings the door wide and smiles. For a moment, I'm rocketed back to memories of my childhood, when I was a little girl raised by a widower who couldn't cook. Inez had taken pity on us and began the weekly tradition of dinner at the Rodriguez house so she could "fatten me up with a home-cooked meal."

"Dee Marie, come in, come in!" Inez takes my elbow in her soft little hands and brings me into her home, then she wraps me in the best hug I've felt in years. Rooster and the guys at the station are huggers, and I love them for it, but no one has ever been able to top Inez Rodriguez when it comes to the art of the hug.

I have to bend a little so she can wrap her arms around my shoulders. That's nothing new. I've towered over her since my growth spurt at twelve. With my chin resting on her shoulder, I close my eyes and allow myself to absorb the affection before we eventually pull apart, and she drags me the rest of the way into her home.

It's the first time I've been inside this place in years. In a town as small as Krause, it's literally impossible to avoid running into your ex-boyfriend's mom, but I've given it the old college try, keeping my relationship with her cordial but distant.

To be here now, with my elbow in the grasp of this sweet lamb of a woman as she draws me deeper into a lion's den of memories and heartbreak, it's terrifying. And it smells so damn good!

Little has changed here in the time I've been away. Inez's soft mauve sofa and chairs sit exactly where they always have, and the bulk of the photos on the walls are familiar, maybe a few new ones of Inez's grandbabies. Inez and Emmanuel's wedding photo still hangs in its gilded frame between a large crucifix and the television. Now, that's new. The old boxy, cathode-ray tube television has been replaced by a large, flat-screen version. A gift from one of her sons, I'm sure.

The delicious scents in the air grow stronger as Inez delivers me to the doorway of the kitchen, gives me another hug, and winks. "I'll get out of your hair, let you two talk." And then, she's out the door, leaving me alone to stare at Rico's back. More specifically, I stare at his broad shoulders, which pull at the soft cotton of a gray T-shirt, and the way his jeans hang low on his hips, the worn denim hugging the globes of his tight ass so perfectly—

This was a mistake.

It smells too good here. He looks too good here. I want to be here too much.

Arriving early was a serious miscalculation. I'm at a disadvantage. With his mom's assist and this glorious view of his ass in those goddamn jeans, Rico has taken the high ground. I'm already losing, and the fight hasn't even begun.

Still I stay, my feet fixed to the floor as I watch the way his shoulder muscles shift when he stirs something in a skillet. I can't help but grin at the sight of him bobbing his head to the rhythm of an old Mariachi tune playing on the transistor radio, which still sits on the windowsill above the kitchen sink.

From the little radio, one of the band's singers lets out a jubilant grito between verses, and Rico howls along with him.

I chuckle, truly enjoying this sight before me. But the sound comes out louder than I'd intended, and Rico jumps right out of his skin, nearly dropping the spatula as he turns to find me there.

"I, uh… I didn't hear the door." He looks all around the room, clearly confused. Grabbing a dish towel to wipe his hands, he checks the clock. "I wasn't expecting you until eight."

"Bold of you to expect me at all." I hold up the bottle of wine I brought with me—because I have manners, even if this is dinner with my ex. "Glasses?"

Rico nods, grabs two glasses from a cupboard and a corkscrew from a drawer. It's all where it's always been, unchanged. While Rico and I grew up and grew apart, everything else here remained the same. He gestures for me to hand him the wine, but I swat his hand away and grab the corkscrew. "You tend to your meat. I've got this."

Rico grins at my accidental double entendre, and his dark eyes shine hypnotically in the overhead incandescents.

I turn away, my attention on the cork in the bottle. When I have a glass poured for each of us, I set his out of his reach—why make it easy for him?—and start walking around the room nursing mine, looking at the old family photos and ornate crosses adorning every inch of the place.

It is so much the same, the same faces staring out at me from these hallowed walls. Some of the faces are family long gone but never forgotten. Like Rico's father and a few of his uncles. Others are faces that have grown, changed, but here on the wall, they stay the same, frozen in a beautiful time. There, included near the center of it all, is a shot of me, playing soccer with Rico and his brothers, Javi and Manny Junior, around the old oaks in this very yard. A sip of wine helps me swallow the lump in my throat.

Behind me, Rico turns the music off, and the silence is as oppressive as the heat he's cooking up in this old kitchen. He clears his throat like he's about to say something, so I jump in first.

"How are your brothers?" I stare at their smiling faces in a photo taken with their dad out at Muleshoe Bend.

I glance at Rico when he doesn't answer immediately. His posture is stiff as he wraps up dinner. "Good. They're good. Javi is in Miami, writing scripts for a telenovela on Univision, and Manny is in California, at Edwards Air Force Base. He was just promoted to Technical Sergeant."

I already knew all that. It's a small town, so how could I not? Then again, I didn't know about Rico's *daddy* news, did I?

Rico clicks off the burners on the stove and carries the food to the table. I watch, not offering to help as he sets the table, lights a couple of candles, and pulls a chair out in front of one of the steaming plates of food.

The candles are a dirty trick, and he knows it. Also, holding out my chair, really? I scowl at him.

Because I'm a brat, I go to the other chair, pulling it out and sitting. He raises a brow, then takes a seat in the chair he was holding. We don't speak for a moment as I take in the spread of food.

Fajitas, my favorite, he remembers. I reach for the tortilla cradle between us and pull out one of the warm tortillas. *It's homemade.* Inez's homemade tortillas are incredible, legendary, literally the only tortillas I've ever tasted that were better than the butter variety from HEB's bakery. I'm in heaven and don't even care that the soft flour disk is burning my palm as I load it full of strips of meat, sautéed onions and peppers, cheese, and pico de gallo. When it's heaped full, I take a big, messy bite.

Oh. My. God. Homemade Rodriguez fajitas, where have you been all my adult life? Right. You've been here, the place I've been avoiding ever since Rico mailed that awful fucking letter to me from Afghanistan and broke my heart—

"Dee—"

"No," I hold up the hand not clutching my fajita and glare at him, "No talking until after dinner."

Rico looks like I've offended him. *Too bad, bucko.* To turn the screw a little tighter, I pull the air horn out of my purse and set it beside my glass of wine.

"What's that for?" he asks, frowning.

"In case you try anything, Drew will hear this and—"

"Oh come on, Dee Dee. You know me. I wouldn't—"

"I don't know you at all!" I try to temper my voice as I add, "And stop calling me Dee Dee. I'm not that girl anymore."

He opens his mouth to argue, and I wag my finger at him. "What'd I say? No talking until after dinner. This conversation is ruining the food. After I've swallowed the last bite, and only after, will I permit you to speak. You will have fifteen minutes to explain yourself, so consider what you plan to say."

If scowls could talk, his would be shouting up a storm right now, but he does as instructed, and we eat in silence. It's unbearable, a little like torture, with nothing but the sound of utensils scraping plates, mouths chewing food. I wish he'd left the music on.

But I've committed to this as my plan for the evening, and I will not back down now. So I focus on the food, enjoying every pop of flavor and burn of spice. I hum with orgasmic delight as the soft dollop of homemade guacamole cools the heat on my tongue and lends its own tang to the mix of flavors.

Only when I've chewed and swallowed my last bite do I settle back in my chair, pour myself a second glass of wine, hug it close to my chest like it's armor, and say, "You may speak now."

Rico's lips twitch, like he wants to laugh at my take-charge approach. I try—and fail—not to notice how the low lights of the candles dance with mirth in his dark eyes. I turn my gaze to my wine, watching the merlot swirl at the bottom of the glass as I wait.

When he's silent for a moment, I raise my gaze and remind him, "You have fifteen minutes. Clock's ticking."

Finally, he dabs a napkin at his lips, leans back a little, and says, "I fucked up."

I blink, waiting for more. *Expecting* more. Is that seriously all I get after all this time? "Explain," I demand.

With a deep, heavy sigh, he finally does. "I was a stupid kid with big ideas about the world, all the things I wanted to see and do. My brothers were having all these amazing adventures in Hollywood and the Air Force, and I wanted an adventure too. I didn't want to be the one Rodriguez boy who never left Krause."

He doesn't say it, and I'm pretty sure he doesn't mean it, but all I hear is: *I didn't want to settle for you and your little small-town life.* It cuts deep.

"So I joined the Army, and they dumped me in Afghanistan. It was hell. In one month, three soldiers from my platoon were killed by IEDs."

I frown, horrified.

"When John, my LT, died, I tried to save him. Tried to keep him from bleeding out after his vehicle hit an IED on the road outside Kandahar. And I lied to him while I did it. I told him we were close to the field hospital. I told him to hold on. He tried. He fought death. It was a struggle. It hurt him to hold on. And in the end, it didn't matter. He still died."

Rico closes his eyes and huffs out a deep breath. After a moment, he opens his eyes again, focusing his dark gaze on me. I try not to fidget under his scrutiny.

Even as a boy, Rico always had a way of looking not just at me but inside me. And now, those eyes pierce through my layers of armor, deep and intense. I look away, down at my wine glass, tracing my finger around the rim.

"A few nights later, when I was released from the field hospital, I went out and stared at the stars and knew with every fiber of my being that I would be the next to die, or the one after that, and I came to terms with it. I found peace in it, and I promised myself, when it was my turn, I wouldn't struggle. I'd let death take me."

Holy—

"The only regret I had about dying was hurting you."

Shit.

"So I wrote that letter to release you. I thought if I broke your heart before I died, it would hurt you less." He clears his throat and takes a deep sip of wine. "I let you go because I didn't want to hurt you by dying. I loved you, Dee, so much. I've always lo—"

"Stop! No!" I pick up the air horn and threaten to blow it if he tries to finish that sentence. "You don't get to say that word, not after everything you *haven't* said to me for *seven fucking years*. You clearly don't even understand that word."

"I understand—"

"Because if you did, then you wouldn't have *stayed* away. How long have you been stateside? And in all that time, you never came to find me. You thought you might die, but you didn't. You survived the war and still stayed dead to me. Why? Why, if you cared *so much* about me, did you end a lifelong relationship with fewer than five hundred words in a letter home from the front and never once look back?"

Now he looks down, unable to maintain eye contact as he says, "Things got complicated."

Complicated. Complicated?

"Complicated how?" I ask, sounding as irritated as I feel when he doesn't elaborate.

"Complicated because...I didn't die. Complicated because...I met Theresa. Complicated because...she got pregnant."

The sound of her name and the gentle way he says it puts a deep ache in the center of my chest. Turning the hurt into anger, I say, "She didn't *get* pregnant. You *got* her pregnant. Own your role."

He blinks at me, then slowly nods. "We got pregnant. And everything changed."

I have questions, so many questions. But I have no energy to ask them and even less energy to hear his answers. I need a break, and I need distance from this man who used to be *my* Rico, from this house that smells like every wonderful memory I have from those days before the war.

I set my wine aside and stand. Giving him a hollow, toothless grin, I say, "Thank you for your honesty."

Then I leave.

CHAPTER 6
RICO

"What the fuck?" I rocket to my feet and follow her out Mom's front door. She has her arms wrapped around her stomach as she walks fast, double-time, to her car. She's running away from me. But I'm not finished. *We're* not finished talking. "Dee, where are you going?"

"Home," she says over her shoulder as she fumbles with the keys to her car. It's last year's Dodge Charger SRT Hellcat, and it's purple. I grin at her choice of vehicle. It's so *her*—flirty and fierce.

But when I speak, all I do is argue. "After all that, you have nothing to say?"

She pauses, turns slowly, and gives me an empty expression as she calmly explains, "I agreed to listen. I've done that. Now I'm leaving."

Without thinking, I stomp over to her, closing the distance between us, and stop too late, when I'm too close. She has to look up to meet my eyes, and the sweet scent of her shampoo on the evening breeze envelops me.

She smells so good, just like I remember. My mind fills with memories of those long-ago summer nights, sneaking out of my window to be with her. Sighs and whispers between us, stolen moments of intimacy that were the foundation of our love life together. The memories hurt, and my desperate need to touch her stings me like venom from my fingertips straight to my heart.

But I can't touch her. I don't. And when she swings her car door open between us, I take a step back.

I'd hoped coming clean with her would open a dialogue, start a conversation, allow me the opportunity to apologize and make amends. But she's giving me nothing. And why should she? I'm owed nothing. She didn't even owe me the courtesy of listening, but she did. Who am I to expect anything more from her?

I stand there, resigning myself to this fate I set in motion on an awful night in Afghanistan. Back then, I'd made a choice. And choices have consequences. Watching her leave me is my consequence.

I squint into her headlights as they stretch across the yard when she backs down the drive, and it feels like the space I put between us all those years ago cracks wider, fissures spidering out to form a deep divide between us.

But she stops. Or rather, she slams on the brakes, puts the car in park, and kicks her door open, coming at me like a charging bull, all huffy and mad. "No, you don't get to do that."

I blink, confused. "Do what?"

"Look all sad and aggrieved with your soulful eyes and your hangdog expression like *I'm* the one who broke *your* heart." Now this is the Dee I've known all my life, *loved* all my life. "*You* did this to *me*. I've done nothing wrong."

"I know."

"You don't get any high ground here. That's mine. You take the low road. You…you… Asshole!"

As much as I want her to get this out, to give me what she feels I deserve—and I do deserve every word of it and worse—she's yelling very loudly, and that worries me for other reasons. I glance across the yard to my brother's old house, the rental where Drew and Chloe are staying, where my son is enjoying an evening playing with their cats, and quietly beseech Dee, "Come back inside, please? I don't want Matty to hear us fighting. He's had enough of that."

Dee's face falls, a stricken look of guilt clouding her expression. She glances around at the night surrounding us and speaks in little more than a whisper when she says, "I don't want to go back in there." She looks past me toward Mom's house. "It's too much…history. Can we walk instead?"

"Of course."

I'm surprised, honestly. I didn't think she wanted to talk to me at all, but that's Dee for you, always full of the best surprises. So I follow as she reaches into her car and shuts off the ignition before closing it up, and we meander down Mom's driveway to Lazy River Road.

We head left, farther up the hill. It's a stretch of road we've walked countless times together, arguably more haunted with memories of Dee and me than Mom's house. All those times as kids racing each other to the creek and shooting cans off fence posts with my BB rifle. And then, those times as teens when we'd come out here for a moment alone in the darkness, fumbling toward a new kind of love under the boughs of Old Man Fogler's live oak tree. This time, there will be no cover-of-darkness make-out sessions, no fumbling toward anything except maybe—hopefully—some version of restored friendship.

We walk slowly, side by side, Dee with her arms crossed tightly over her chest, me trying to stay loose, approachable, ready to listen to her side of this mess I made.

The moon hangs low in the sky, glistening off the shards of tall prairie grass flanking the asphalt road. Stars blanket the darkness, blinking and winking and falling all around us.

This view of the sky is second to none. Even in the darkness of an Afghan winter night, no vision of the universe there ever felt quite as glorious as this view of the cosmos from home. Still, I looked up, spotting familiar constellations, taking in the wonder of the universe. It made me feel connected to this place, even as I was set adrift by war.

Somewhere in the distance, a coyote cries out, and soon another responds, connecting in the dark. Dee's steps falter. She always loved the call and response of the coyotes out here, listening closely to the notes of their howls like she was deciphering the lyrics of some song, a love ballad.

Now, their song sounds too sad, too lonely. And as we're serenaded by this lost love ballad, Dee turns to me and asks, "Where is Mateo's mom now?"

I close my eyes, not wanting to talk about Theresa. But this is the most important part of anything I tell Dee. She can't forgive me until she can trust me, and she'll never trust me if I don't tell her everything. So I answer her on a gust of breath, like I have to force the word out of me. "Prison."

Dee blinks one moment, and her eyes go wide the next. She wasn't expecting that response, but who would? After my dad's stroke and Dee's mom's overdose, my mom and her dad struggled as widowed parents, but they both managed to provide stable homes for us kids. Prison, let alone jail, was never a reality for us, and thank God for that.

Dee stares up at me, patiently waiting for more.

So I give it to her. "She was in my platoon. Injured in the same attack that killed my LT. I think I started to care for her and look out for her to make amends to John. I couldn't save him, so I would save her... Though, in the end, I failed her too."

Dee frowns at me and looks away, down at our feet planted a few paces apart on the blacktop, which is still warm from the day's sun. I don't know how much detail she expects from me, so I start talking, expecting she'll cringe or blow her air horn when she wants me to stop.

"When she returned to duty, we got closer. Then..." *Here we go.* "One night, I was feeling lonely and sorry for myself, and...it happened."

"*It happened.* What, like osmosis?"

Fair point. I need to own my mistakes if I ever want her to forgive me for them. "I got drunk. We had sex. I got her pregnant."

"Why didn't you use protection?"

"I did." I cringe. I can't believe I'm talking to the love of my life about whether I used a condom when I fucked another woman. "It broke."

She groans and rolls her eyes, but it's the God's honest truth.

I change the subject. "We tried to make it work. I barely knew my dad before he died, and I didn't want that for my son. So we...tried. What I didn't know at the time was she'd developed an addiction to pain medication." Dee cringes, and I pause, knowing I've touched a nerve in reminding her of the addiction that took her mother. But I need to get this all said, so I push forward. "There was a lot I didn't know about Theresa, and when we tried to have a relationship, it was…not good. Looking back, I realize trying to form a family with her was the worst decision I could have made. The only thing Theresa and I have ever had in common is an amazing son."

Clearing my throat, I continue, "She managed to stay clean while she was pregnant. I'm forever grateful for that. But shortly after Matty was born, she relapsed. I was deployed in Afghanistan while she was stateside with Matty, strung out on God knows what. One day, she left him locked in a hot car in the Walmart parking lot. Fortunately, a shopper spotted him, and the police shattered the window to get him out."

Dee looks appropriately horrified because it *is* so fucking horrifying. I shiver at the thought of what could have happened that day. Mom sends Christmas candy to our Walmart-parking-lot hero every year now.

"That was the first time Theresa went to jail, and Matty was placed into foster care. I was granted a Chapter 5-8 discharge from the Army, and once I was back home, I petitioned the courts for full custody of Matty. Theresa was allowed supervised visits as long as she stayed sober, but she couldn't.

"When Theresa tried to steal meds from one of her elderly neighbors, she was arrested for robbery and assault. The courts took away her visitation, and I was allowed to move Matty here. Now, I just want to give him the life he deserves, a calm and comforting home where he can thrive." I finally stop talking and watch Dee as she soaks up everything I've told her.

After a moment, Dee nods sagely and says only, "Thank you for your honesty."

Not that again. It's her kiss-off line, her signal she's about to leave. She turns away from me, walking back toward the house, and I follow, working to keep pace with her fast strides. After a good hundred yards, she stops and swings around to face me, her expression one of anger as she huffs, "What I still don't understand is *why.*"

"Why what?"

"Why you left me to go fuck someone else."

"That's not why I—"

"I know you think you left for some noble reason. You left to 'free me' or some bullshit, but did you actually believe that breaking up with me would make me stop loving you?"

Oh God, what a thing to say. Those words are sadder than any coyote song. I stare at her, dumbstruck. She turns and storms away. Jogging to catch up, I nearly run straight into her when she halts and turns on me again.

"Did you never feel that way for me? Because if you had, it wouldn't have been so easy for you to leave."

"It *wasn't* easy—"

"You thought you could spare me by hurting me? Jesus Christ! What is wrong with you?" She scowls at me, and the hurt in her eyes breaks my heart. A lump forms in my throat, making it impossible to speak as a single tear trickles from the corner of her eye and traces down the soft slope of her cheek.

She takes a moment, and when she speaks, it's barely more than a whisper as she tells me, "If you'd died, it would have broken my heart...*again.* Even after you'd broken my heart the first time, I still would have mourned you. So don't act like you were being noble, sparing me from caring. I've always cared about you. I *still* care about you, you fucking asshole. I can't help it. And I hate it. You left me, but you didn't die, and I hate you for it."

Another tear escapes, and Dee angrily brushes it away.

Fuck. It was a lot easier to hurt her from eight thousand miles away. Standing here, watching the tears fall down her cheeks, I want to make it better, make it right between us again, and fix this awful mess I made.

Without even thinking, I hug her. It's all I know to do. It's all I've ever known to do with Dee. When she's hurting, I hug her. It's rote. But the moment my arms wrap around her and pull her against my chest, I know it's so much more than habit. It's the first connection I've felt with her since I left for war all those years ago.

For a moment, one brief, perfect moment, she lets me hold her. She lets me take a deep breath of the scent of her skin, her hair, and I feel her body melt against mine, surprisingly soft for such a strong woman. A breath saws out of her, and I squeeze her even tighter.

But then the moment ends, and she pushes me away. With one mighty step backward, she glares at me. "What is this? What are you trying to do?"

I play dumb. "Hug you?" While it's stating the obvious, it's not entirely true. The moment she melted into my arms, I knew I'd want more, *need* more from her, *with her*. I'm desperate to fix what I broke between us, to earn her trust again. I want to get back everything I could have had with her if I hadn't been such an idiot.

Like she can read all my thoughts in my eyes, she shakes her head, and her sadness turns to anger, a fire sparking deep within. But she doesn't yell at me. She looks past me to the horizon where the road dips back down toward my mom's house, and in a painfully soft voice, she says, "This was a mistake." And with that she brushes her tears away and adds, "This can't happen again."

Itching to fight about this, I challenge, "Why not?"

She frowns at me, like I've reached a new level of stupidity for not understanding. And maybe I have, but I want her to explain it to me. I need her to talk to me.

She doesn't though. All she says is, "Goodnight, Rico." Then she leaves me again, walking double-time down the hill.

This time, I don't try to match her pace. I let her leave me, keeping an eye on her from afar as she makes it to Mom's house, gets into her sexy purple muscle car, and takes off down the hill toward town.

When the glow of her taillights disappears into the night, I groan with exhaustion and walk to Drew's house. I'm about to knock on the door when I hear my son's laughter inside.

Opening the way in, I catch sight of him and that bright red cast covered in graffiti as he runs through the living room with a wand in his hand, trailing a string with little feathers on the end. Two bumbling cats come rolling and rollicking after him as they give chase.

It's a beautiful sight, watching my son's joy, and his laughter is the best sound. I take a moment to revel in it, soak it in. I have a lot of regrets in my life, but having my son is not one of them. He's single-handedly taught me how to find joy, even on the bleakest day.

"Daddy," Matty squeals when I pick him up and spin him around. The wand with the feathers spins with us, and the cats go bonkers trying to catch them. "Can we have cats?"

Oh Jesus. I set him down, trying to pick my words carefully as I say, "Well, we'll talk about it. But I don't think—"

"You're always welcome to come over here and play with Bodhi and Utah, kiddo." Chloe is there for me with the assist.

Over Matty's head, I mouth, "Thank you." To Matty, I say, "Tell everyone thank you for dinner and goodnight, big guy. It's your bedtime."

He gushes his thanks and gives Drew and Chloe hugs, then turns his attention to the cats, trying to capture and kiss each of them while they squirm away. Finally, I clasp his hand in mine to move him out the door.

"Did you have fun tonight, buddy?" I ask once we're outside, meandering between the oleander and crape myrtles that separate Drew and Chloe's rental from Mom's house.

"Yes," Matty answers matter-of-factly. Then adds, "I love cats. We need cats."

I bite my lips together to keep from smiling. "Do we now?"

Matty nods resolutely, like it's settled, a known fact, and I know this won't be the last I hear of it.

"My darling daughter!" Dad croons, already sounding drunk at eleven in the morning.

At least he's consistent. Between the hours of 10 a.m. and 2 a.m. I always know where to find him: right here, perched atop the third stool from the left at his favorite bar, The Rusty Bucket. Someday, when he dies, surely the good folks at the ole Bucket will retire his stool or add a memorial plaque or something.

I wrap my arms around his middle and hug him as he pats my hands and asks, "Tell me, sweet girl, are the rumors true?"

I avoid the question as I saddle up to the bar on the stool beside him. Only when Polly, the bar's owner, sets an iced tea in front of me, do I speak. "What rumors?"

A couple of Dad's grisly old barfly buddies chuckle. Dad does, too, his beer-soaked breath coming out in a hacking laugh. "Don't give me that. You know what I mean."

Of course I do. I'm sure the ole rumor mill is churning out the guff in record amounts over this latest town news.

Did you hear, our Deidre Fletcher went on a date with Ricardo Rodriguez?

Oh my word, isn't that something. Do you think they'll finally marry?

"Word is you're dating little Ricky Ricardo again."

I grin at Dad's old nickname for Rico. It's been years since I heard him use it—and Rico is hardly "little" anymore. It makes me nostalgic for the days when Dad was younger and more sober, and I was young, dumb, and in love.

"That's absurd. Who's spreading these lies?"

"Inez."

Of course.

I roll my eyes and steal a hot wing from Dad's basket after Polly sets it in front of him, along with a fresh beer.

"She said you came over for dinner the other night, and it was very intimate." He waggles his fluffy, gray eyebrows as he passes me the ramekin of blue cheese dressing for my stolen wing.

"Dinner doesn't equal dating, Dad. I have dinner with you all the time!" I hold up my hot wing as proof—though, technically, this is lunch.

"And you're the love of my life, Deidre Marie." He kisses my cheek with a sloppy smack, then dunks his chicken wing in blue cheese and takes a bite.

For some reason, this admission from Dad reminds me of Rico. It's remarkable—and a little disturbing—the resemblance between their situations. Both married to drug addicts they didn't love and both working to raise a child on their own. But Mom's death broke my father in ways I never understood. Still don't.

Rico, on the other hand, seems stronger than ever, resolved to give Mateo a good life. And, with his mom to help him, I have faith he'll succeed. For Mateo's sake, I hope he does.

Chewing his food between words, Dad asks, "So you and Ricardo, is it a *thing*?"

"No, it's not a thing." I toss my stripped chicken bone into his basket and wipe my fingers with one of the napkins Polly delivered in a stack. "And the people of this town need to mind their own business and stay out of mine."

Dad sips his beer, and, trying to sound wise, he says, "The people of this town want to see you and Ricardo back together again."

"Well too bad because *they* don't get a say in my relationship with Rico."

"Aha, see, you just admitted it's a relationship."

I roll my eyes and steal another wing as I spin off the barstool and head out the door. "Later, Pops!"

"Stay frosty, little firecracker!" Dad hollers to the back of my FIRE T-shirt, and his friends all wish me well as I step out into the blazingly bright afternoon sun, chewing the meat off the wing bone as I cross the street to the firehouse.

"There she is!" Rooster's deep baritone voice rumbles up through the rafters of the apparatus bays to announce my arrival on shift.

I toss my chicken bone in the trash, scoring a three-pointer, and celebrate with a little dance, bragging, "Nothing but net."

Watts acknowledges my shot with a disinterested nod as he messes around on his phone. Drew ignores me completely, busy checking over his turnout gear for today's shift. Rooster doesn't seem impressed either.

I stand there, staring at the tops of their heads, waiting for the inevitable hazing, the torrent of poor-tasting jokes to rain down upon me, but nothing happens. Unlike everyone else in this damn town, my fire crew does not subject me to harassing questions and intrusive assumptions. And that's just one more reason to love my boys.

After a bit of idle chatter, Watts directs us to the station's meeting room, where we review rope and rescue knot techniques for different swift-water rescue scenarios. And it's so boring.

These slow days at the station are the worst. They leave too much time for thinking, and today, all I can think about is Rico. Which pisses me off.

Up until now, I'd done a decent job of keeping my mind off him, avoiding thoughts of our dinner and our stroll up Lazy River Road. I'd emptied my mind of the memory of the old oak tree on Jonas Fogler's farm. The way its wide spindly shadow shimmied in the breeze, black against the brilliant blanket of stars.

That had been *our* tree, claimed by our initials when we were kids.

That tree saw our first touches, our first kisses, our first... So many firsts. It was also the place where I suffered my first heartbreak, the day Rico told me he'd enlisted in the Army. Like a sixth sense, I'd known, even then, he was leaving me.

The other night, the sight of that tree had stopped me in my tracks. I'd stood there in the center of the blacktop, the day's baking heat radiating into me through the soles of my shoes, melting me to the spot. Stuck, staring at the one place in this entire universe that held more memories—both terrible and wonderful—than any other.

I'd nearly burst into tears, but Rico saved me. Without even knowing it, he stepped in my way, forcing my attention away from the ghosts of our past. I'd stared up at him, the boy I used to love, all grown up into a man I didn't know.

Then, he'd hugged me, and it felt so good, and he smelled so good —too good. It was all *so good* it hurt, smarting like a thousand bee stings straight to the center of my chest. So I'd left him there, on that hill beside our old tree.

A dispatch alert chime sounds throughout the station, and Doris the Dispatcher's voice rings over the announcement radio. "Attention Engine 31, Attention Medic 3, need to respond to 4227 East Elm, Unit B. Caller indicates seventy-five-year-old female suffering heat-related illness."

"That's Margaret's apartment," Watts murmurs as we all come to attention and rush to the bay where Engine 31 waits.

All of us love our engine, but I'm chauffer, and Number 31 is my girl, my fire-engine red, screaming she-bitch from hell. I drive her with a vengeance, like I have something to prove. And maybe I do. When I was at the fire academy, some asswipe suggested women were too weak to handle this much power. I'd proven him wrong when I mastered driver training while he washed out of the academy.

Drew and Rooster clamor into the cab, and Watts takes his spot at shotgun as I crank up the engine. With a quick check of mirrors, I hit the gas, and we rumble forward to the end of the station driveway as Watts hits the siren. I put my shoulder into a left turn, and we race toward Elm.

The drive is a short one, and with a squeal of our air brakes, I set us at the curb in front of Margaret's apartment complex: Stonehaven Court. It's a collection of four squatty buildings, six units in each: three up, three down. Margaret and the other elders tend to fill the ground-floor units to avoid the stairs. Margaret's apartment is front and center, a prime location for gossip and socializing, and right now her porch is crowded with worriers and onlookers.

We move seamlessly on scene, each of us well versed in the tasks of our roles. I strap on my radio unit while Drew and Rooster grab the paramedic gear. Watts communicates with dispatch, checking on the status of EMS as we assess the situation.

Due to the advanced age of many of the Stonehaven Court residents, we get called out here a few times a week, and Margaret is one of our frequent flyers. She calls 911 anytime she hears a strange noise or a neighbor burns dinner. Once, when her cable went out, she called 911 asking us to use the ladder truck to check the connection at the pole. This time, though, the tone of conversation in the crowd surrounding Margaret's door suggests this is not a false alarm. Something is wrong.

The screen door opens with a metallic yawn, and I hold it so the guys can file inside before following. The air in Margaret's apartment is stiflingly hot. While outside it's a breezy ninety-five degrees, inside it's got to be triple digits.

It's crowded in here. Neighbors linger, looking concerned, while one woman uses a damp washcloth to cool the back of Margaret's neck as she sits on her couch, looking rose-cheeked and wilted from the heat.

Rooster and Drew act as the EMTs on scene while we wait for the ambulance to arrive. Watts and I see to crowd control, clearing the room of all these extra people so we can work. When it's just the five of us, I turn my focus toward investigating the source of the problem.

"Margaret, sweetheart, why is it so hot in here?" I ask while Rooster wraps a blood pressure cuff around her arm, and Drew checks her pupil sizes and reactivity with a penlight.

"ACs broke," Margaret says, sounding thick-tongued and lethargic.

"How long's it been broken?" I twist and turn the knobs and dials on the thermostat, checking for reactivity too.

The screen door clatters again, heralding the arrival of EMS. They drag a gurney with them into the tight space.

It's too many cooks in this very hot kitchen, so I step outside onto the crowded porch, aiming to find the AC condenser and investigate the malfunction. But my forward progress is blocked by a wall of muscle when I walk right into Rico.

It's like déjà vu all over again. The smell of him, the feel of him, just like that evening, a few nights ago, when he had me in his arms, his hand clutching the back of my head, gently stroking my hair as he enveloped me in his scent, his warmth…

And now, it's happening again. Thick, strong, corded arms with the sleeves rolled up to the elbows band around my waist as I bounce off his solid chest.

All conversation, all movement, everything on this porch and in the known universe of Krause, Texas, stops to watch as we teeter, awkwardly tangled together. When I don't fall on my ass, I look up at my savior, staring for one brief, glorious moment into those deep, dark eyes before I shimmy out of his embrace. Murmuring, "Thanks," I weave through the crowd to escape everyone's attention.

There is a beat of silence before Rico's deep voice speaks. But his words aren't directed at me; he's speaking to Mildred, the town librarian and a resident here at Stonehaven. "You say she hasn't had AC for weeks?"

"Well now, let me recollect…" Mildred's reply is slow in coming, and soon I'm out of earshot, walking around to the back of the building where a bank of air compressors sit in a neat little row on a concrete pad surrounded by weeds.

I find the unit marked B for Margaret's apartment and focus on that one, popping open the breaker box to make sure nothing tripped or fried. It all appears fine. Squatting, I start pulling weeds, in case any have grown up into the machinery, but that doesn't seem to be the source of the problem either—

"Hey."

I jump at the sound of Rico's voice behind me and lose my balance, pitching forward and hitting my head against the condenser unit. "Jesus!" I come up, whining and scowling and rubbing the sore spot on my forehead. "Warn a girl next time you're sneaking up on her."

"What girl? I only see a woman here." Rico's smile is wickedly innocent and irritatingly casual, like we don't share decades of good, bad, and ugly history together. Like I'm just some random *woman* he's flirting with.

I scowl at him harder, and the fool has the nerve to chuckle about it.

Seriously? Of all the scenes at all the emergency calls in all the world, why did he have to walk onto mine?

"Why are you here?"

"Press," Rico says and flashes his *Krause Gazette* ID badge.

I laugh. "Press? Really? Are you here to talk to Martha Mitchell about Watergate?"

He smirks. God, I *hate* that damn sexy smirk. "I was in the area and heard your unit called out—"

"Oh Jesus, what, are you stalking me now? You best not be stalking me, Ricardo Ignacio Castro Rodriguez, or I will string you up by your scrotum in that tree over there." I point to a decorative elm for clarity. "Don't doubt that I will."

Now Rico really smirks, looking more annoying than sexy as he continues his statement like I didn't just threaten him with genital torture. "I heard your unit called out to Stonehaven Court, and I followed to see if it's another case of elder abuse."

I blink. "Elder abuse?"

"Yes, some of the elderly tenants have complained about the landlord charging them for expensive repairs that he never completes. I'm doing an exposé. Did you know Margaret's air conditioner hasn't worked right all summer, and despite daily calls to apartment management, she still sits in a sweltering hot apartment every few days?"

"I—" I look down at the bank of air conditioners, most sitting idle. "Shit."

"Yeah."

The radio at my waist crackles to life with Watt's voice. "Dee, we've handed over the scene. Heading back."

I stammer a bit, staring up into Rico's eyes as I listen to Watt's words. Rico is like a magician with those eyes, casting some spell to make me useless to the rest of the world, all my focus on him.

With a deep breath, I break the spell, look away, and take a step backward as I answer into my radio, "Copy." Then I turn and leave.

Matty comes running at me, and I narrowly avoid getting beaned in the brain by his big, red cast. He swings that thing like a cudgel when he hugs me.

"Hey, buddy, how was school today?"

"It was awesome! We got to learn about butterflies."

"That does sound awesome!" I don't remember ever loving school as much as this kid does. His excitement is a joy to behold. "Tell me everything."

He does, going into great detail about how wiggly little caterpillars grow wings and fly around.

As he talks, I drive, taking him from the school to the hospital, just a quick stop before we head to the house. In the parking lot, I find an open spot, then wait for Matty to take a breath so I can ask him, "Hey, little man, do you mind if we visit a friend in the hospital?"

"The hospital?" Matty peers up at the building. "Did he break his arm too?"

I grin. "No, *she* got a little overheated today, and the doctors are checking her out."

Matty nods, and I reach into the passenger seat to retrieve the bouquet of daffodils—I'm told they're Margaret's favorite. Once I have him out of his car seat, I hand the bouquet to Matty, giving him the important task of carrying them to Margaret. He takes the job seriously, clutching them between his cast and his good hand. I guide him with my hand on his head, and we go inside to the front desk. Soon, we're escorted back to her recovery room. There, Margaret is stretched out on an adjustable bed, a game show playing on the television.

"Ms. Everly, my name is Ricardo Rodriguez, and this is my son, Mateo."

Margaret blinks at me, then watches Matty as he walks to her bedside and holds the flowers out to her.

"These are for you," he says, lisping a little where he's missing a tooth on the left side.

Margaret accepts the flowers, giving them a sniff before speaking to Matty. "Thank you, young man. They're beautiful. To what do I owe the pleasure of your visit?"

She directs the question to Matty, but I know she's asking me, so I respond, "I'm with the *Krause Gazette*. I was wondering if you'd be willing to answer a few questions."

"Questions about what?"

"About your broken air conditioner."

"Do you always bring your child with you to interview people?"

"No, ma'am," I grin bashfully, trying to play up my charm, "but his grandma has church this evening, and I wanted to chat with you. Do you mind?"

"Not at all." To Matty, she says, "Would you mind pushing this button to get the nurse's attention? Let her know I need a vase and water for the lovely flowers you've brought me."

Matty mashes the call button over and over until a nurse appears in the doorway. Margaret smiles at my son as he relays her instructions to the nurse, and we get a hospital jug and some water for the flowers. Once that's settled, I pull up a chair, and Matty sits on my lap with a coloring book I brought for him.

"Some of your neighbors tell me your electricity hasn't worked quite right for the last few months, and now your air conditioner is on the fritz too."

"That's right."

"And apartment management won't do anything about it. Is that correct?"

Margaret pulls a face, looking self-righteous as she launches into a rant. "That family calls themselves Christians, but they wouldn't know a bible if it hit 'em in the head. And they sure don't take care of the people who are paying to live in that complex. I tell you, the problem is with that Curtis fella. As soon as the family put him in charge, it all went to heck in a hand basket. He's always cutting corners, saying things are fixed when they ain't."

"Like what?"

"Like my AC! Three whole weeks ago, that Curtis fella came around asking me for five hundred dollars to pay for repairs to my air, and have I seen him since? Not a once!"

"You shouldn't have to pay anything for repairs. That's the responsibility of the apartment complex, not the tenants."

"Well, I don't know about all that."

I scribble notes furiously, boiling with anger that the Smith family, in particular their spoiled son Curtis, is fleecing these elders. Repairs are not the tenant's responsibility. That's one of the benefits of living in an apartment.

"Do you know of other repairs they're not correcting or charging tenants for?"

"Well, my lights flicker funny sometimes. I've mentioned that to Curtis, but he ignores me. Pamela upstairs—her kitchen light just plumb stopped working. It's not the bulb. It's the whole dang light. Plus, there's ants everywhere. I've got 'em coming out of the sockets in the walls. And I tell Curtis all this, but does he care? Oh no."

As Margaret rants, the nurse returns to Margaret's room to announce, "The doctor is ready to sign your release papers, Margaret. Do you have a way to get home?"

Margaret pauses, considering, so I'm quick to offer. "Matty and I can give you a lift home."

She smiles softly. "I'd appreciate that, Ricardo. Thank you."

In a hurry, I move Mateo off my lap so I can lend a shoulder for Margaret to lean on as the nurse helps her into a wheelchair to leave the hospital.

When she's settled in, her daffodils clutched on her lap, I take Matty's hand, and we keep pace with Margaret's wheelchair out to my car. Once I have her comfortably strapped into the passenger seat and Matty in the back, I get in and explain that I'm going to make a quick stop at Walmart. When we're there, Margaret stays in the car with the AC running while Matty and I hurry inside and buy a small window-unit air conditioner for her apartment. Once we get her home, I take a few moments to install the new unit, and Margaret insists on cooking us dinner.

It's too late in the evening to knock on doors, asking the neighbors about their repair problems, but over a dinner of spaghetti marinara—the cool breeze of her new AC blowing over us—Margaret outlines exactly who lives where and various maintenance issues they've experienced in their units. She even shows me a journal she's kept of everyone's complaints, as well as check stubs of her payments for various incomplete repairs.

"May I borrow all this?" I thumb through her meticulous notes.

Margaret nods, seeming proud of her role. And she should be: Margaret is my Deep Throat on this story, the perfect source. With a few confirmations, my elder-abuse exposé is practically written for me.

I'm bubbling with excitement for all the good I can do with this story. But it will have to wait until tomorrow. Matty is starting to yawn, which means he's about ten minutes away from whining incessantly about everything and nothing. It's bedtime for my boy.

Thanking Margaret for dinner and the leftovers she packed up for us, we head home. I keep the leftovers in the car—mamá would never forgive me if I put another mom's cooking in her fridge—and usher Matty through his bedtime routine of teeth, prayers, and stories. This is my favorite time of the day, when it's just Matty and me, lying side by side on his bed while I read *Guess How Much I Love You* to him, again. Twice.

It's our book, the one I would read to him over video calls when I was deployed and he was alone with his mom, stateside. Now, together, we both seem to get something from sharing it in person too.

When I finish the second round, I look over to find Matty sleeping. With a kiss on his forehead, I turn out the light and leave the door cracked open, the hallway light on, just the way he likes it. It didn't take him long to settle in and feel safe at mamá's house, and that hall light keeps the nightmares away, so it stays on.

"Why do you smell like garlic?" mamá asks as she comes in through the back door and hugs me.

It's best to be honest. "I took Matty out to dinner." It's mostly honest. I change the subject. "Mamá, do you mind keeping an ear on Matty for me? I thought I'd go into the office for a few hours to get some work done."

"Of course, mijo," she says, and I hug her again before I head out the door.

Dan finds me at the copy machine, making my own copies of Margaret's notes and check stubs so I can return her originals. "What's this?" he asks as he holds up the leftover spaghetti. I'd put it in the break-room fridge with a note on it: "Free to a good home in a hungry stomach." Glad to see it's found one.

"Spaghetti, courtesy of Margaret Everly," I say as I move back to my desk with the bundle of originals in one hand, copies in the other.

"I mean this." Dan sets the air conditioner receipt on my desk.

"It's for a window unit for Margaret."

He smirks. "And the paper needs to pay for that, why?"

Defensively, I try to justify the expense, pointing at my piles of papers. "She's given me a lot of information for this story, and I drove her home from the hospital tonight after she suffered heat exhaustion. I couldn't leave her to cook in that apartment another night."

He smirks again. "I'm not the one you've got to convince. This goes on Franklin's desk in finance."

I groan.

He grins. "Good luck."

The emergency scanner on the corner of my desk crackles to life, a woman's voice speaking, "Attention Ladder 12, Engine 12, Engine 31"—that's Dee—"need to respond to structure fire at 4227 East Elm."

Ice shoots through my veins at the sound of the address.

"Isn't that—?" Dan starts.

"Margaret's building," I finish and quickly stand, grabbing my go-bag—an old backpack that holds two bottles of water, snacks, my camera, recorder, press ID, lots of pens, and a notepad.

"I hope she's okay," Dan says to my back as I sprint for the door.

"I hope they all are."

CHAPTER 9
DEE

We can see the fire from blocks away. Orange flames spike into the black sky, gray smoke billowing above, cinders raining down between the silhouettes of tree branches. It calls to us like a beacon, leading us back to the scene we visit far too frequently.

This time, when we arrive, I stop near the hydrant so Rooster and Drew can run hose to it, then park about fifty feet from the structure as they charge the hose. Ladder and Engine 12 line up at the curb, and their crews do much the same thing.

Watts is incident commander for this scene, coordinating our attack with the other crews, while I interview witnesses lining the curb and milling around in the street. Soon, I have a list of two residents unaccounted for: Pamela on the second floor, unit D, and Earl on the ground, unit A.

After informing Watts of the situation, it lands on Drew, Rooster, and me to perform search and rescue for Pamela on the second floor, while the guys of Engine 12 look for Earl down below. Ladder 12 gets to work venting the building and getting water on the roof.

Drew and Rooster lead the way upstairs with the hose, attacking the seat of the fire, and I follow in their wake, a torrent of sooty runoff water rushing over my boots and down the stairs. The fire hasn't reached the front of Pamela's unit yet, but the air up here is thick with smoke, reducing visibility to just a few feet.

Using my flashlight to see through the dense smoke, I crouch low, where the visibility is better, and search for the missing woman. I check the couch and chairs in the living room, but, more often than not, it's the floor where we find survivors. It's usually where we find the dead too.

And I have found more dead than I'd care to remember. It's the worst part of the job. On those difficult days, I wonder why I chose this career. In high school, I'd planned to go into emergency medical services. I wanted to help people, to *do something* the next time I walked into a room and found a mom overdosing. Then I got that shitty letter from Afghanistan, and now I help people by running into burning buildings.

Go figure.

Pamela is easy to locate, curled up in the bathtub with the water running and a wet towel over her nose and mouth to keep the smoke out of her lungs. I crouch beside her, trying to assess any injuries. She looks unharmed, though her pupils are blown, her eyes bouncing around the room, looking past me toward the doorway, probably wondering if she's still surrounded by fire.

"Can you walk?" I start to help Pamela to her feet.

"Leroy!" she screams over my head as she balances on shaky legs, her feet slipping a little in the wet tub.

"Who's Leroy?" I ask her, ready to inform the team we have another potential victim or survivor up here.

"Leroy!" She howls at the ceiling and hacks as her throat seizes up.

I manage to get Pamela out of the tub and into the main hallway, where Rooster and Drew are keeping our exit clear of fire.

"My baby!" She starts shouting again, her voice raw and scratchy. "He ran away when I tried to bring him into the tub with me."

What baby could *run away*—?

"Is Leroy a dog or a cat?" Drew steps in to ask.

"He's a Bichon Frise."

Of course. Leroy is a dog. Why didn't I think of that?

"Get her out of here. I'll find Leroy," I tell the guys.

"Dee, no, these trusses won't hold—" Rooster tries to argue, but I cut him off.

"I'll be quick."

He cusses at me as he picks up Pamela and starts to carry her outside. Drew cusses at me, too, as he directs the hose's stream down the hallway ahead of me, trying to knock down the fire at the back of the apartment, where I'm headed. On the radio, Watts is cussing me now as well, but I'm compelled by the desperate look in that woman's eyes. I need to save Leroy for her, and maybe a little bit for myself too.

Search and rescue for animals is different from search and rescue for people. This time I look under the furniture instead of on top of it, crouching to peek under tables and beds.

With Drew attacking the fire from inside and the ladder crew outside dousing the flames that burned away portions of roof, everything that's not actively burning is damp and steamy. Torrents of water pour through holes in the ceiling like sooty gray waterfalls. Charred beams and rafters creak and groan from the stress of the fire and the weight of the water.

In the main bedroom, the sheets on the bed are charred, turned to an ashy paste where the fabric spontaneously ignited from the heat. And beneath the bed lies Leroy. He's on his side, his white fur now gray from the smoke and soot. He's not moving, and my heart sinks. *Please be okay, little Leroy, please.* A stubborn streak works through me as I get down on my knees and pull Leroy out of his hiding place.

"Leroy!" I yell at him, hoping for a response. I don't get one, but I do detect a faint, fluttery pulse. Awkwardly, I cradle the little dog in my arms and move back onto my feet, ready to hustle us both out of this building.

That's when I hear it: the snap, the crackle, the dreaded pop. The sound comes from over my head. I have enough time to look up as a portion of the ceiling gives way, charred beams and the remnants of soaked Sheetrock and insulation raining down like an avalanche.

Adrenaline burns through my veins as I move, filling my head with the deafening roar of blood pumping faster and harder, making me feel stronger, untouchable. With Leroy pressed against my chest, I dive across the floor out from under the collapse.

I make it, mostly. Debris pelts my helmet and back, but it's nothing I can't handle. However, the pain that shoots through my ankle and up my leg takes my breath away.

As the dust settles, my radio squawks, Watts instructing, "Engine 31, it's past time to get out of there."

I agree, one-hundred-percent, but when I try to move my left leg, pain shoots through me again, and the debris pinning my ankle to the floor won't budge. I respond to Watts, "I'd like to, but I'm stuck."

"Received." Watts's voice is loud and clear as he stops all other radio chatter with the announcement: "Fletcher of Engine 31 is calling a Mayday. She's on the second floor, Delta side. We've got a Mayday, Mayday, Mayday."

The Mayday tones sound over the radio. There is nothing more frightening than that sound, which indicates that a firefighter is trapped or injured. A shiver blasts through me as I realize that, this time, it's me who's trapped and injured.

"Emerson, report," Watts instructs after the tones.

"Partial collapse of the ceiling onto her legs." Drew's voice filters over the radio, and I turn as much as I can to see that he's here in the room, assessing the ceiling.

Relief washes over me at the sight of my fire brother. *I might be injured and trapped, but I'm not alone.*

Drew keeps talking to Watts as he tests the weight on the debris pinning my leg. "Remainder of the ceiling appears stable, but I'm going to need some help lifting this off her and the dog."

Right, the dog, the reason I'm here. I look down at little Leroy in my arms, shielded beneath me. He's still lethargic and unresponsive despite our traumatic tumble. I radio to command. "Prep the pet med kit too. Leroy needs some good air."

Within a matter of seconds, Rooster comes bursting into the room, Kramer from Engine 12 right on his heels. Drew and Kramer put their dead lift practice to work, pulling the beams and debris up enough that Rooster can grab my gear and yank me out from under.

Blood rushes back into my ankle and foot with pins and needles, and I wince at the sharp pain. Rooster hands Leroy off to Kramer, so my crew can focus on me, quickly examining the condition of my injury before Rooster wraps one arm around my shoulders and slips the other under my knees, lifting me like I weigh nothing, like I don't practice my dead lifts right along with them in the station weight room. He carries me while Drew grabs the hose, and we make egress.

The indignity of being carried out of a fire I walked into hurts worse than my ankle. I complain loudly, assuring Rooster I can walk fine on my own. He ignores me, and rightly so. I'm lying. My foot doesn't feel like it's there. No pain, no tingles: there's just nothing.

Concentrating for a moment on my legs as they bounce against Rooster's arm, I try to *really feel* my foot. There's no sensation. Jesus, is it gone? Did it get torn off by the falling ceiling?

With a peek over Rooster's elbow, I'm relieved to see both of my boots bobbing with his steps. "Oh good," I say and smile at him when he frowns at me, looking confused. I explain so he'll understand. "I'm glad my feet are still attached."

"She's a little loopy," Rooster says to the paramedics as he delivers me to one of the ambulance gurneys in the street.

Without Rooster's bulky shoulder blocking my view, I look all around at the sea of curious onlookers, everyone strobed in the red and blue disco of emergency lights. Nearby, Pamela and Leroy are being tended to. Leroy appears to be awake. Sooty and lethargic, but alive. Hooray.

Behind them, another ambulance hosts an old man with a shock blanket wrapped around him so tight you'd think it were winter in Siberia. Earl from the first floor, I presume.

"He's in shock," I explain to my medic.

"Huh?" he asks, not really listening as he pulls my mask and helmet off and flashes a penlight at my pupils.

Around the blind spot he's created in my vision, I see Drew heading toward our engine. Then Chloe bursts free from the crowd and tackles him with a mighty hug, getting coated with soot as she wraps her arms around him. She must have heard the Mayday call over the radio and come running, thinking it was her man pinned beneath debris in a collapsing building.

"Nope, just me," I mutter as Drew rips his mask off so he can plant a smoking hot kiss on Chloe. Now, I grumble: "Must be nice."

My medic looks up from where he's trying to remove my boot to examine my leg. "What's that?"

"It must be nice to have someone who cares about you."

He frowns at me. And…

Wait. I squint at him. Oh God, I know him, like, in the biblical sense. John, that was his name. *I think.* My memory is fuzzy from that night, but I'm pretty sure he's the medic I took home after a night of Darts & Drafts with the guys at The Rusty Bucket. I'd hit on him that night because he was exceptionally good at darts and had a wicked smile. I remember the sex was good, but that was over a year ago, and I can't recall if he stuck around for breakfast. John is still frowning at me, and I'm not sure if it's because of my incoherent ramblings or the awkward memories of our one-night stand.

I turn away from the judgment I'm sure is in John's eyes and farther from Drew and Chloe's public display of affection, looking for someone else to focus on. Anyone else.

That's when I see him, that familiar face, a face I once knew better than my own, a face I once loved with all my heart. I watch with confusion as Rico comes running at me, looking every bit as worried as Chloe looked when she tackled Drew. And for a moment, just one moment, I let myself imagine that someone *does* care enough about me to worry. That *he* cares enough to come running.

And then he's in front of me, breathing hard and staring at me with those deep, dark eyes. Rico comes as close as he can without inter-fering with the medic, reaching for me, his fingers taming my tangled hair, stroking my neck, his thumb tracing a soft line across my cheek.

I blink up at him, completely entranced by his eyes and the soft way he's touching me. Like he's pushing a strand of hair out of my face, over and over again, his fingers stroke behind my ear. It used to be his spot, where he'd caress sweetly after we made out under our tree. It's hypnotic and erotic, and it's messing with my head.

Rico is the only man—or boy, for that matter—who has ever been sweet to me. Everyone else sees my armor. They know they can be rough with me, so they are. Rico, though, is gentle. He touches me like I'm breakable, and he never wants to break me.

Leaning down to my level, his gaze so intense it's like he's staring into my soul, Rico asks, "Are you okay?"

No. I'm not okay. I haven't been okay for a long time. But right now, staring into the depths of his eyes, I feel...better.

The logical part of my brain tries to reason with me: *It's the adrenaline. It's making you confused. Don't fall for his strange Rico magic.* But the look he's giving me right now—such affection and caring, such total relief to be at my side—it's too powerful. It's the look I'd longed to see all those years ago when he would have come home from the war, ready to start our life together.

There's a part of me that fills with rage: Why did I have to wait so long for this? But another part, a bigger part, is overwhelmed with the desperate need for more. His fingertips caress me, but I need his hands, his lips, his whole body.

So I let myself forget everything else. The apartment fire and the chaos of the crowded scene fade into the background. I turn away from our complicated past and unknown future so all I can see is him and me, right here and right now. I let *everything* go when I grab the front of his shirt and yank, pulling him to me and mashing my lips against his.

Rico seems confused, frozen in place, but that passes quickly, and then he's tightening his fingers on the back of my neck, pulling me against him as his mouth melts to mine, his lips softening as he kisses me for the first time in too long. It's so different, yet so much the same.

Rico still tastes like I remember, but he's a man now, and he kisses like a man, not a boy. When he takes the kiss deeper, his tongue doesn't beg—it demands entrance. And I gladly give it. He brings a second hand up, cupping my cheek, his fingers tangling in my hair, and I clutch at his shirt, feeling the rigid muscles of his chest as I hold on. God, he's hot, and his kiss is volcanic, hotter than the fire I just came out of. I'm melting into him, completely pliant to his hands, his mouth, his warmth.

"Dude! What the fuck? Get off her!"

Confusion washes over me at the sound of sharp voices. I blink my eyes open to see Rooster yank Rico backward.

The sudden shift in our situation surprises Rico too. He keeps his eyes fixed on me, ignoring Rooster as he catches his breath, his luscious lips swollen from my kiss.

"Wait." Rooster is staring at me, too, looking more confused than Rico. "Dee, did you want him to…?"

He doesn't have to finish his question, and I don't have to give him an answer. He knows. We both know. Everyone here knows. Yes, I wanted his kiss. I've always wanted his kiss. But as soon as I recognize that reality, I remember the other reality too. Rico hasn't always been gentle and kind and good to me. I might be tough, but I'm still breakable, and I just kissed the asshole who broke my heart.

"Fuck," I say as I wipe my mouth and frown at Rico. I glance past him and all around at where the whole town is watching. And, insult to injury, there's my actual injury. John, still busy doing his job, checks something with my ankle, and I yelp in pain.

"Let's get you to the hospital," John says.

I nod and studiously avoid eye contact with Rico and everyone else as they wheel me into the back of the ambulance and shut the doors.

"Fuck!" I yell up at the ceiling, feeling helpless and weak and stupid.

I can't believe I just kissed the only man who ever hurt me. Worse than that, I just kissed him in front of *everyone*. And, worst of all, there's this lingering urge inside me to do it again.

The ambulance leaves, and I stare at the empty space it occupied moments before. My eyes fix on the spot where Dee blew my mind with a kiss.

"What do you think you're doing?" The brawny redheaded guy looks as red as his hair, fuming with rage, and from the sharp expression in his eyes, it's obvious his rage is meant for me. It's cool that he's so protective of Dee. I'm glad she has someone looking out for her. But I wish he didn't feel the need to protect her *from me.*

"She started it?" I defend myself, meekly.

"What are you, five?" It's another member of her crew who says this from behind me. I turn to face off with a Black man who somehow manages to tower over my tall frame.

"To be fair, she did start it." Drew lends me support, only to turn on me an instant later when he joins the chorus of puffed-up men and adds, "But if we hear one word from Dee that you've hurt her again, you will regret it. Are we clear?"

I consider defending myself further. I want to explain the situation to them, except I don't actually understand the situation myself. And anything I have to say now just sounds pathetic, even in my own head. So I simply acknowledge Drew's warning. "I understand."

At that, the three men temper their aggression toward me, uncrossing their axe-wielding arms and nodding as they walk away, back to their truck to pack up the hoses and gear. One by one, the fire trucks extinguish their lights, like they extinguished the fire, and with the hiss of air brakes, they return to their stations.

The last of the ambulances leave, too, heading back to the hospital, some transporting patients, some mercifully empty. All that remains are police, volunteers, onlookers, and displaced residents. I take a few photos and interview some witnesses, including Margaret. Someone brought a chair so she'd have a place to sit, but it's a small consolation considering all her possessions were destroyed tonight.

When she finishes giving her statement to a young officer, she looks at me and says, "Looks like the new AC you bought me couldn't cool down the apartment after all."

"How are you doing, Margaret?"

"Oh, you know, I'm alive." She doesn't sound exactly happy or relieved about that, mostly exhausted.

"Are they finding you a place to stay tonight?"

"Oh yeah, some of the parishioners at my church are organizing rooms in their homes for us to stay for a little while."

"Good, I'm glad—"

"What are you still doing here? Shouldn't you be at the hospital with that girl of yours?"

"She's not my—"

"Coulda fooled me. Now get going!"

"I… Uh… Okay. I'll be back out here in the morning. You take care, Margaret." I lean in to kiss her cheek before leaving.

On my drive across town, I check in with the news desk—aka Gary—and relay my brief story to him so he can publish it online tonight. Tomorrow, I'll reach out to the fire investigator for details about the fire's cause, then write a more in-depth piece to publish with my photos in our weekly.

Once we hang up, I call my mother from the car, too, staring up at the hospital as she answers. "Hola, mamá, have you heard about the fire?"

"Sí, mijo, it's terrible news." Of course she's heard about it. Her ear is always to the ground, knowing the town's news sometimes before it happens.

"Well, Dee was injured as she rescued a resident."

"¡Ay dios mio!"

"Not seriously, it looked like maybe her ankle was broken. But I'm going to go to the hospital now and sit with her." *If she'll let me.*

"Por supuesto."

"I might be out all night. Do you mind keeping Matty overnight?"

"Don't be silly. Of course I don't mind. And we'll be by in the morning with breakfast."

"Mamá, you don't need to bring—" I glance over at the call display to see that… "She hung up on me. And now I'm talking to myself."

With a deep centering breath, I linger in my car for a moment longer, staring at the hospital entrance, trying to collect my thoughts.

It's been a long day. I'm exhausted.

It's been a weird day. I'm exhilarated.

From the panic and adrenaline rush of the fire to the ecstasy of that kiss… God, that kiss.

I lick my lips like I can still taste her there. But it's just a memory now, like all our other kisses.

Dee'd been my first kiss. She was my first *everything.*

I learned *how* to kiss with Dee. More importantly, I learned how Dee liked me to kiss her, and I hadn't forgotten those lessons. This kiss, though—it had been wholly different. Why?

People change, I know that; we grew up. When Dee and I were teens, we kissed like teens. We were learning about ourselves and each other; kissing was an exploration, an adventure, a desperate, breathless advancement toward some mysterious future life.

This kiss wasn't about adventure or advancement toward some distant horizon. This kiss obliterated the horizon, like an atomic bomb boiling the air around us as our lips collided, our tongues tangled, an inferno burning between us, stoked hotter with every taste.

This kiss was, without a doubt, the sexiest kiss of my entire life. And I want more. But what does Dee want?

With a groan, I climb out of my car and slam the door closed. Inside the hospital, I consider a cup of the lobby coffee, but it looks like motor oil, so I take a pass and head to the front desk, where I aim to sweet-talk my way into Dee's room.

Janet at the front desk lets me in, and I find Dee sleeping peacefully in her little bed, her left leg immobilized in some sort of contraption. I guess I thought she'd be awake, interested in talking to me or at least interested in fighting. To come into her room and find her asleep feels like a violation. I turn to leave, but I'm hemmed in by a nurse who's come for her nightly rounds, checking Dee's vitals and fluids.

Dee stirs awake and blinks past the nurse toward me. She doesn't say anything, and neither do I; we just stare at each other as the nurse adjusts the saline drip. Once she leaves, I half expect Dee to tell me to leave, too, but she doesn't. She doesn't say anything.

Dee's eyes start to drift closed, like they're too heavy to hold open. Quietly, I settle into the chair beside her bed and turn my head to watch her, ready at any moment to leave when she demands it. But she never does.

⎯ᴧᴫ⎯♡ᴧᴫ⎯

"I was broken, too, but they fixed me."

That voice. It sounds like my son.

"They're going to fix me today. Maybe I should get a red cast to match yours."

And that's Dee.

"Then we can be twins!" My son squeals at a pitch so high it makes me twitch.

"Shh, you'll wake the sleepyhead," Dee whispers loudly.

"Daddy *is* a sleepyhead. Sometimes I have to jump on him to wake him up."

Dee's laughter sounds like music, a siren song that pulls me from what's left of my slumber. I shift, and pain lances through my neck and shoulders. Grimacing, I blink my eyes open and find myself sprawled awkwardly in a chair in the corner of a hospital room, surrounded by people.

Dee's dad, Mark, stands by the window, backlit by the bright Texas sun, looking far older than his age. Mamá is here, too, laying out food —enough food to feed an army—on a counter below the television set. And she has an army to feed, what with Dee's fire crew all here, watching me with suspicion again. At the center of this impromptu party, Dee sits high in her adjustable hospital bed, one arm draped over my son's shoulders, the two of them gossiping about me, apparently.

"Daddy, you're awake!" Matty says even louder than his terrible attempts at whispering.

"Yep. Yep. I'm up." I squint as I rub the sleep from my eyes and sit a little straighter in the chair. I try to smooth out the wrinkles from my shirt, but it's no use. I'm a rumpled mess and still reek of smoke from the fire.

"You snored really loud!" Matty proclaims with delight.

I blink at him. "I did?"

"You sounded like a pig," he announces then starts to make oinking sounds.

Dee howls with laughter and hugs Matty a little tighter against her side.

"Dee Marie," my mom interrupts, pointing at an empty plate and the spread of food before her. "¿Qué te gusta comer?"

Dee shrugs. "I'll eat anything, Mrs. R."

Mamá loads up a plate full of pastries, fruit, and tacos, way more food than Dee could probably eat in a day. When she hands the plate over, Dee winks at Matty. "What do you say, Mateo? Wanna help me eat all this?"

Matty nods and grabs one of the tacos. I wince, worried he'll make a mess, but Dee doesn't seem to mind, so I let it go. Mamá serves heaps of food to Dee's dad and her fire crew next, serving me last.

"Do the nurses know you're feeding their patient?" I ask as mamá hands me a plate laden with tacos, cantaloupe slices, and a pumpkin empanada.

"Está bien," she waves my concern away, "comes, mijo."

She's speaking Spanish more than English this morning, which means she's upset. And from the way she sets my coffee down a little too hard, sloshing some over the rim, I'd wager she's upset with me.

Why? Because I stayed out all night? I wouldn't blame her if she resents being used as a babysitter while I spent my time falling asleep beside my ex-girlfriend. Come to think of it, I owe mamá an apology.

But not right now. She's busy fluttering around the room, taking care of everyone here, pouring refills of coffee, stacking second helpings onto a few plates, making sure we all have enough napkins, and feeding the entire nursing staff on this floor.

I hardly have an appetite, but mamá will worry if I don't eat something, so I polish off one of the tacos and the empanada before I set my plate aside. Dee and Matty finish what's on their plate, too, and manage to fend off mamá's offer of second helpings.

An awkward silence falls over the room as everyone seems to sense it's time to talk, but what are we supposed to talk about? The very air in here is charged with emotions, memories, anxiety. They dampen the conversation.

Finally, Dee interrupts the silence. "Inez, would you mind taking Matty to the bathroom so he can wash his hands? He's going to get me all sticky with his cantaloupe fingers."

To soften the blow of this expulsion from the room, Dee grins at Matty and pulls a face. When he acts like he's going to smear his sticky fingers in her hair, she dodges and weaves and sticks her tongue out at him like she's six years old too.

Mamá attacks Matty's fingers with a wet wipe from her purse. Then she takes his hand and helps him off the bed and out the door in search of a restroom for a more thorough cleaning. There is a bathroom in the room, so it's clear mamá and Matty's quest is a guise. Dee's other guests sense that, too, and find reasons to leave, kissing her on the cheek or wrapping her in big bear hugs as they go. And soon it's just her and me, alone again.

I brace myself for a torrent of anger from Dee: anger that I'm here now, anger for the years I wasn't, anger about that spectacular kiss last night, anger about, well, *everything*.

Instead, she says, "I'm sorry."

I blink. "*You're* sorry?"

"Yes, I kissed you without your consent last night. That's not okay."

I come to my feet, advancing closer to her. "I was more than okay with—"

She holds up her hand to stop me from coming any closer. "Rico, last night was a mistake. I was in a weird headspace, high on adrenaline. I wasn't thinking clearly, and I shouldn't have done what I did. It won't happen again."

I hate this speech, but I let her say it. I know she needs to control this, whatever *this* is. I controlled our breakup. If we're ever going to come back from that, it needs to be her who decides it, drives it.

But that doesn't mean I can't help things along. I give her half a grin. "Dee, if you ever want to kiss me again, you have my complete and total consent."

She narrows her eyes at me. "And speaking of consent, I never said you could come into my room last night. I was asleep—"

"I'm sorry—"

"Who do you think you are, strutting into my life after all this time and pretending to care?"

"I do care."

"Don't interrupt me."

"I'm sorry."

"You made your choices, Rico. You left me to go to war, and then you left me again. You started a whole new family. And now you think you can walk back into my life like nothing happened? You expect me to just be here, waiting? No. I reject that. I reject you. It's my turn to dump you now, so consider yourself dumped."

"Okay."

"Okay?"

I nod.

Dee looks surprised I'm not arguing, her brow furrowing adorably. "Well. Good. You can leave my room now."

"May I speak first?"

"Why?"

"Because I have something to say."

Dee grumbles, but she gives me a moment to talk.

I use my moment efficiently, saying what's at the top of my mind. "I never stopped loving you."

Dee groans. "You married another woman."

"I fucked another woman and got her pregnant, so we got married. There's a difference. She hates you, by the way, calls you 'the ghost' because you haunted our marriage."

Now she's really frowning. "Don't blame me for—"

"I'm not blaming you for anything. It was all me. I fucked it all up. I left my heart with you. I was the one haunted by you. I still am. I could never stop thinking about you, missing you. Every single morning since the day I shipped out, your face is the one I want to see when I wake up. But you've never been there because… I'm a stupid fucking idiot, and I'm filled with regret.

"And worse than any of that, I hurt you. And I can't take it back. I can't undo it. You were my person, you know? From the time I was eight, you were the person I cared most about in this world, and I hurt you. And I hate myself for that. I regret it with all my heart." Shit. I'm tearing up. I sniff and tuck the emotions away as I say what I need to say. "I know I don't deserve anything from you. I don't deserve your love or your friendship. I don't even deserve your time. But I'm begging you for it. I just want to be in your life again, in any way you'll have me. If all you need is a friend, I can be the best fucking friend you ever had—"

"Shut up!" she yells as tears wet the corners of her eyes. She rubs them away, and her voice turns to an angry whisper. "You weren't just my best friend, Rico. You were everything. I had *no one* but you. And then you were just…gone."

Fuck. I hurt her, so much. And I hate myself for that. I broke both our hearts, beyond repair. Rubbing my eyes and wiping my nose, I try to maintain eye contact as she stares at me, her eyes peering through me.

After a moment, she speaks again, saying, "I want you to leave. And I want you to leave me alone."

Feeling raw and ripped apart, I wipe more wetness from my eyes and turn to go.

"Your mom and Matty can stay though."

I nod, grinning just a little at that. Out in the hall, I worry that Matty and mamá, who look concerned, heard some of our conversation. I crouch and give Matty a hug. "I need to go to work today, buddy. I have to write about last night's fire. But we'll hang out tonight, okay?"

Matty searches my face with worried eyes.

I give him a wide smile, trying to hide behind it as I nod over my shoulder toward Dee's room. "Take care of her, okay, big guy? And don't forget to sign her cast."

Mamá encourages Matty to go into Dee's room while she stays out in the hall with me, that stern-Mom-look on her face. "What are you doing, mijo?"

"I love her, mamá. I always have. Last night cemented that for me."

"Don't you hurt her again, Ricardo Ignacio Castro Rodriguez. ¿Comprendes?"

"I'll do everything in my power not to. If anyone's going to get hurt this time, it'll be me."

"Which worries me too."

I'm not sure what to say to her. I can't promise anything. I broke two hearts with that awful letter home from the front. Is there still a chance to mend us both, or are we broken beyond repair?

Every Sunday, the *Krause Gazette* publishes their weekly paper. Thick with coupon inserts and local news, it's the only print item they put out. Like most small-town newspapers these days, the *Gazette* can't afford to print more than once a week, but it's a "weekly with a website"—as they like to call themselves—and I've been on that website every day for the last two weeks, reading every single word Rico writes.

Earlier this morning, the print edition hit my door with a *thump*, and I unfolded it over the kitchen table so I could read Rico's headline story as I ate my breakfast. It was another installment of his in-depth exposé into negligence and fraud at the Stonehaven Court apartment complex. In the two weeks since the fire, he's managed to uncover countless incidences of mismanagement, as well as neglect of safety concerns and maintenance. Turns out, the fire that resulted in nearly two million dollars in damages and displaced seven residents was caused by ants. I've known for some time that ants can be a major fire hazard when they swarm electrical equipment, but I've never seen it so spectacularly illustrated before the Stonehaven fire.

I've learned a lot about the fire from Rico's stories. Like, how the landlords ignored multiple complaints from tenants experiencing electrical problems, some even reporting ants coming out of their wall sockets for months before the fire. Calls to exterminators and electricians could have avoided the near-fatal incident, but those calls were never made. And for their negligence, the building's owner and manager now face criminal charges and multiple lawsuits.

Rico is a superb journalist. He manages to convey information about complex legal matters and archaic building code bylaws with efficient, clear language without boring his readers. I didn't know he had such a talent for writing. Sure, his letters home from the front had proper spelling and grammar, but he's grown into quite the eloquent wordsmith since—

"Ricky Ricardo sure is a talented writer, ain't he?" Dad elbows me in the side, and I try to surreptitiously fold The Rusty Bucket's copy of the *Gazette* back up and push it away from me.

"He's all right." I shrug.

"Uh huh." Dad chuckles.

I groan and turn back to the bar, waiting anxiously for Polly to pour me a new pitcher of beer.

If the folks in this town—including my father—could stop with this wink-wink, nudge-nudge routine, that'd be great. But, alas, no. Everyone in these parts has an opinion about my fiery kiss with Rico, and they all see cartoon hearts in the air when it comes to little Deidre Fletcher and their favorite hometown hero back from the war.

When Polly finally slides the pitcher in front of me, I blow a kiss to Dad, then manage to carry the beer one-handed, working my crutch with the other, as I hobble back to the corner where my crew have paused our darts tournament for refreshments.

It's obviously killing Rooster not to help me with my load, but he's wise enough not to try. And I manage fine on my own; there's minimal spillage as I distribute my contribution to Darts & Drafts night with some of the guys from the station and a few of our EMS compatriots.

John, aka Mr. One-Night-Stand Paramedic Guy, is here. And it's awkward how Rooster keeps waggling his brows at me, like he's ready to act as wingman and help me get laid. On a normal Darts & Drafts night, I'd be game, but tonight, my thoughts are elsewhere. My thoughts are where they've been for the last two weeks, centered firmly on Rico. While I've been recovering from my injury and learning to manage on crutches, my traitorous mind keeps looping back to the night of the fire. Not fixated on the scary moment when a ceiling came down on me. Oh no. It's the kiss I can't forget.

Mr. Unforgettable Lips has done exactly what I asked of him: he's left me alone. But my imagination has been less cooperative. Every night in my dreams, he comes to me. His lips against mine, his hands clutching, needing, taking what he wants, pulling me closer, holding me tight, and never letting me go. It's amazing and awful.

Once I've poured everyone a fresh beer, I set the empty pitcher aside and collect my darts, ready to get some of this frustration out by throwing sharp objects at the wall. But Rooster scares the crap out of me when he loops a lanky arm around my neck and pulls me against his side.

In a whisper loud enough to be heard over the music, he tells me, "Listen, doll, heads up. John the Paramedic has eyes on you and questions on the tip of his tongue."

I groan.

"Is that going to be your answer to his questions?"

"Probably." I try to shrug Rooster off me, and he just leans heavier onto my shoulders.

"It's a wonder you're so popular with the boys. But listen, why not consider answering in English instead. You could say something like, 'Thank you for asking, handsome, but, you see, I can't fuck your brains out tonight because the love of my life is back in town, and I'm working up a good angsty lather for him.' "

I groan louder and dip out from under Rooster's weight, hopping a little to balance on my good ankle as I turn and threaten him with one of my darts. "You're in the danger zone, buddy!"

Rooster laughs and starts singing the Kenny Loggins song. I ignore him and all the other guys, focusing on the dart board. I put all my feelings there, all the anxiety and confusion, those lusty wet dreams, and my residual anger and heartache; they all fill the board. Then I aim and throw. The first dart hits the triple seventeen, putting me on the finish to win this tournament of 501. I aim my second dart at the triple twenty and hit it, much to the cussing and consternation of my opponents. With my last throw, I take a deep breath and exhale slowly as I aim, throw, and hit my mark, winning the game.

Rooster crows and pulls me into another smothering hug. The guys on the other team pat my back good-naturedly and wave at Polly to serve the round of shots we'd wagered.

After we've all thrown back our whiskey, One-Night-Stand John comes over to me, and it's time to nip this in the bud. With a smile, he leans in a little closer, but I speak first.

"Hi, John. So listen, I had fun with you all those months ago, but that was a one-time thing. I'm not looking to connect again. Okay? Sorry."

John blinks at me, then bashfully points past me. "I was just trying to get to my phone."

I glance down at the table littered with empty glasses and pitchers, and there beside me is a phone in a rugged black case. "Oh."

"Sorry." He shrugs. "I'm seeing someone."

"Oh." I nod and smile like a possessed doll. "Cool."

John grabs his phone and wanders off, and I turn away, mortified. There, watching, Rooster collapses against one of the stools in hysterics. So pleased with himself.

"Shut up, asshole. You put ideas in my head."

"You're so easy to mess with."

I grumble.

"Trust me, doll. No one in this town is going to hit on you. Everyone knows your heart is taken."

"It is not!" I protest with a childish pout that I'm sure looks completely pathetic on a grown woman.

"Darlin', if you ever want to get laid again, there's just one guy who can hit the spot for you, and you know it."

"Nope."

"Yep."

"I hate you."

"Liar."

I grumble again.

"You're such a joy to be around."

I'm working up a great retort when the whole bar goes quiet, only the haunting sounds of Merle Haggard on the jukebox echoing through the boxy space. It's like in the jungle when all the little forest creatures sense a predator nearby, and they duck and cover. What the hell is everyone ducking and covering from here—?

Oh.

Across the room, just through the door and glancing around at all the eyes on him, is Rico. I haven't seen him since that morning in my hospital room when I pushed him away. Unlike that morning, his clothes aren't rumpled, and his hair doesn't stick up in little tufts where he slept on it.

He looks…really good, practically glowing in the low light of the bar. He's in an Army T-shirt and worn jeans that fit him so well I have to force my gaze back to less dangerous sights.

"Speak of the devil, and he appears," Rooster whispers to me, but in the hush of the crowd, it sounds too loud. Rico must hear it, too, because he turns his head, and his gaze locks onto mine, his expression one of guilt, full of apology.

Why?

Silently, Rico mouths one word to me, "Sorry," then he turns and leaves. I blink at the blank space he's left in his wake, then look over at Rooster, who's doing the same thing, his eyebrows at his hairline, like he's even more confused and surprised than I am.

I sling my bag over my shoulder and collect both crutches as I swing for the door. Out in the lot, Rico is unlocking his car. I still can't believe he drives the same car as me, only his is black instead of purple.

"Where are you going?" I holler his way.

Rico stops and turns, looking me up and down as I make my way to him.

"Mamá took Matty to church, so I thought I'd come check out the bar I was never old enough to drink in when I lived here. I didn't see your car in the lot, or I wouldn't have…"

Seriously? He's been actively avoiding me? "When I told you to stay away, I didn't mean you'd have to avoid me completely. It's a small town, Rico, so that's pretty much impossible. I just didn't need to wake up in the hospital and find you there. It was…confusing."

He nods, looking sad, and it makes me sad too. He's kept away, just as I asked him to, and I've hated every minute of it. In the weeks since my breakup speech, I've looked for him everywhere, secretly hoping he would challenge my orders. Of course he didn't. Rico's always been the sort of man who respects boundaries, even when maybe I wanted a little nudge over them.

I don't know what to say to him now, and it's hot out here, and the lot's parking light is too bright—it makes me squint and tear up. I gesture over my shoulder and say, "You can come back inside. You don't have to run away from me."

He smirks like I've insulted him, but he says nothing and makes no move to return to the bar.

"I was leaving anyway."

Now he speaks, asking, "How are you getting home?"

Interesting. I figured I'd get a ride home with Rooster, but instead of explaining that, I shrug. It's a weirdly passive expression, not like me at all.

But apparently it says what I need it to say because Rico replies, "Let me give you a ride."

Well, that's a hell of a sentence; a lot's packed into those six words, six syllables. "Okay." I pack a lot into those two syllables, too, and move closer to his car.

Rico hops to attention as I near, hurrying around to open the door for me. It's such a gentlemanly thing to do, and I freeze as I stare at him. Like the chair he'd held for me at our reunion dinner all those weeks ago, accepting this kindness feels loaded with meaning, but I accept it anyway.

I slot my crutches into the wheel well, then I climb in. Rico surprises me when he closes the door behind me, and I start to panic. Jesus, what am I doing? Why did I get in his car? Why am I about to give him directions to my apartment? Why, when we get there, do I know with absolute certainty I'm going to invite him up?

It's like I'm a glutton for punishment, like it's my kink. Hell, maybe it is. My lifelong fear of abandonment has led to other questionable decisions when it comes to men, so why not this one too?

As Rico climbs into the driver's seat, he fills the space with his scent, his big body, and they overwhelm me. I practically purr when he turns the key and the engine growls to life. Quickly, I text Rooster: **I got a ride home.**

He responds almost immediately: **Enjoy the ride, doll.**

I silence my phone when he texts a bunch of eggplant emojis and follow his advice, enjoying the ride.

Rico pulls his Charger into the spot beside Sweet Priscilla, my precious purple girl, then turns off the ignition. I stare at the empty seat he leaves behind when he gets out and shuts his door, then jump when he opens my door and offers a hand to help me out.

For some reason, I accept his help, even smiling a little when he gets my crutches out of the car for me.

Then he asks, "Which one's yours?"

I point to the second floor.

"Not very accessible. I'll help you up the stairs."

I should decline; I've managed these stairs just fine for the last two weeks, but I'm inclined to accept his offer. I think it's his scent; it's fogging up my brain, making me say and do dumb things. As he climbs the stairs with me, I consider all the reasons I should send him home, all the reasons I don't need his help, don't need his proximity. But with his fingers gently set against my back, making sure I don't fall, I can't remember reason at all.

Once we're on my landing, it's time to thank him kindly and send him away. But I keep silent as he walks me all the way to my door and waits while I put the key in and swing the door wide. I step in and feel the relief of the conditioned air, air that doesn't smell like Rico. You'd think it would be enough to clear my head. But the way his Army tee pulls taut across his chest distracts me. Jesus, he's so sexy. I hop a little, like I'm making room for him to enter, a silent invitation. But one of my crutches gets caught on the entrance rug, and I nearly tumble backward.

Rico is quick to reach for me, wrapping one arm around my waist as he helps me steady myself. It's a relief, *and* it pisses me off. I don't need his help. I've never needed his help.

To demonstrate my strength and take the control back, I balance on my good leg and let my crutches fall as I clasp my palms against his cheeks, holding him in place, our lips so close, eyes staring deep into each other. I ask, "That consent still good?"

"Very." His voice rumbles straight through me.

I smash my mouth to his, kissing him furiously. His kiss is furious too. We're a pair of cannibal piranhas devouring each other in a violent, delicious frenzy. I put all my heartache into that kiss, biting his lips, tangling my fingers in his inky black hair, and pulling like I want to hurt him. But not like this. I want to hurt him in much better ways than hair pulling.

Slipping my fingers from his hair, I go for his shirt, trying to tug it over his head, but I wobble on my feet. In an instant, Rico picks me up and carries me to the couch. He sits with me straddling his lap and leans up to press his body against mine as he tugs his T-shirt over his head.

A pair of dog tags clatter as they fall back against his tanned, toned chest. I frown at them, this symbol of his service, the tracker of his life or death in a desert on the other side of the world. A mix of emotions overwhelms me as I stare at them now, like they embody the separation that came between Rico and me.

With that reminder of all that's come between us, I feel the need to remind him too. "This means nothing."

Rico kisses my neck, that sensitive spot right below my ear as he whispers, "What means nothing?"

"This." I sigh as he nibbles my earlobe. "If we're going to fuck, it's just fucking. Nothing more."

Rico licks all the way down my throat to the indentation in my collarbone and murmurs against my skin, "What if I want more?"

I pull back enough to look him in the eyes and smirk. "Tough. This is all you get from me. Take it or leave it."

He reaches up and cups his hand against my cheek so sweetly, too sweetly. I close my eyes, the softness of his gaze too much to bear. I repeat, "Take it or leave it."

After a moment more, he answers, "I'll take it."

Awesome.

My eyes spring open, and I give him a wicked grin as I clutch his dog tags and move them aside, the metal warming in my grip. I kiss the place where they'd lain, right over his heart. Rico's fingers tangle in my hair, like he wants to hold me there. But when I start to kiss my way down his chest, he lets me.

He tastes salty and sweet, delicious. I lick my way down the ridges of his muscles, smiling each time he reacts with a spasm, like I'm tickling him. He leans back as I crawl down between his legs until my knees hit the floor.

Rico watches me, likely wondering where I'm taking this. I'm wondering that too. What the hell am I doing? Despite his acquiescence to my terms, I know this is more than just fucking; we have far too much history for it not to be. This man, whose thighs flex as I stroke my fingers up to unzip his pants, is the only man who ever held my heart and the only man who ever broke it. And here I am, on my knees for him.

This is fucking stupid. I'm losing control of this situation, and fast, but I can't help myself. Rico is a fucking magnet, and I'm iron, helplessly attracted to him. Coaxing his hips up, I pull his jeans and briefs down enough for his cock to spring out, fully erect, weeping, desperate for me. *At least he's helplessly attracted to me too.*

And, God, I love this cock. Rico's is the first dick I ever sucked, and I *loved* sucking it. His responses were invigorating, his hands roamed, clutching, needy for me, and his orgasms were so rewarding, always getting me wet and desperate for him.

Now, I'm better at giving head. I've had more practice. I want to show him. I want him to know what he's been missing. I want that knowledge to sting. Staring deep into those dark eyes, I lick my lips, bend forward, and slide my mouth over his length, sucking him deep to the back of my throat.

Rico's whole body tenses, and his groan sounds feral, like a growling tiger caught by the tail. Hollowing out my cheeks, working his length, I can taste the salt of his pre-cum as I have my way with him.

"Jesus Christ! Oh fuck, baby, yes!"

Baby? No one's called me that since the day he kissed me goodbye at the airport. Even in his letters and calls from the front, he only ever called me Dee Dee. *Baby* was reserved for intimacy. *Baby* was waiting to welcome him home.

Hearing that term of endearment now, after all this time, has a strange effect on me—probably the opposite of what he intended. My erotic energy turns angry, the heat inside me exploding into a burning rage.

I fist his hips with a bruising grip and suck him harder. I use my teeth, scraping up the length of him before I swallow him down again. It's a weird blow job, fueled in equal measure by rage and affection. I've missed him. I've missed his body. And I hate that I've missed him and his body. I hate that I'm enjoying this as much as he is, that I'm dripping and desperate and need to make him come more than I need my next breath.

"Oh fuck! Dee, yes, baby," Rico huffs, and with a groan, he warns me, "I'm gonna come."

His warning only makes me more merciless. It gives me power, and I revel in it. He's entirely within my control. I could stop right now. I could deny him this pleasure, leave him begging. But that's not how I want to hurt him. I want him to know what he gave up when he hurt me.

I jerk him with one hand, squeeze his balls with the other, and swallow his length until I'm practically choking on him. And that's what does it.

His muscles strain and he gasps, "Fuck, baby," as he spills down the back of my throat.

CHAPTER 12
RICO

Jesus Christ.

I shouldn't keep saying that, especially on a Sunday when mamá and Matty are at church, but...

JESUS FUCKING CHRIST!

That blow job was good, scary good. Sometimes more scary than good. And I loved every fucking moment of it. Teeth, who knew? There is something incredibly sexy about being at Dee's mercy, where any moment she could've bitten my cock clean off. But she didn't. And I came so hard I'm still seeing stars.

New kink unlocked? Definitely.

"Jesus Christ," I say out loud this time, stroking Dee's cheek as she rests her head on my thigh, still on her knees on the floor between my legs. God, she's gorgeous, especially now with her hair tangled from my grip and her lips glistening and swollen from my cock. "Where'd you learn to do that?"

I regret the question the instant it leaves my mouth. Dee looks up at me, and the flicker of desire shining in her bright green eyes ignites into an inferno of rage. *Shit.*

She wipes her lips with the back of her hand, like she can't stand the taste of me there, and climbs to her feet, wobbling on the cast as she lets out a hollow laugh. "What did you think? That I pined for you all those years, twiddling my thumbs in some Rico Reject chastity belt? Oh honey, no. I've had loads of men since you. I fucked and sucked my way through Fire Academy. I know half the paramedics in this town and San Antonio, biblically."

When she moves like she plans to walk away, I wrap my arms around her waist and pull her backward off her feet and onto my lap. Then I spread my legs, which effectively parts hers as well.

"Well then, practice makes perfect, baby, because that was the *perfect* angry blow job," I whisper into her ear as I nibble on the lobe.

"Fuck you." She squirms in my arms.

"That's the plan." I tuck my hand inside her pants and palm her pussy. I always loved how turned on she'd get from blowing me, and I love that it hasn't changed. She's dripping, the thin cotton fabric of her underwear completely soaked. I growl like a rabid animal, desperate for a taste. But to clarify, I ask, "That consent still good?"

"Yes." She twists her hips to press her hot pussy against my fingers as her ass teases my cock.

With that one glorious word—*yes*—I pounce, tossing her off my lap and onto her back on the couch beside me. Pushing her top up, I suck her nipples into peaks as I tug her pants down her thighs, taking a moment to carefully slip them off over her cast. When she's bared, I get rough again, pushing her legs apart so I can taste her. *Ah, God, she's so sweet.*

I gorge, devouring her, my tongue pressing inside her pussy as I strum her clit with my thumb. She arches her back, and her tits demand attention from my free hand. She grabs for me, too, clutching my hair and pulling, like she still wants to hurt me. I let her. Perverse as it may be, I like it.

When we were young, we were bumbling and curious, gentle as we explored each other. Now, we know. We've learned. Now, we have years of life experience loaded into our libidos. She's so much wilder now, much more confident and assertive. And I can't get enough of it.

I press a finger into her pussy, and she gasps. I pull it out and take a taste, then replace the one finger with two, finger fucking her as I tease her clit with my tongue.

Her sighs turn to moans as she tries to top from the bottom, twisting her hips up to ride my face and fingers at her own pace. But I'm in charge now, and I have my own ideas about how this will play out. I let go of Dee's tit so I can clamp an arm over her hips, holding her still, keeping her at my mercy. She writhes against me as I build her pleasure higher and higher at a steady, rhythmic pace.

It's when her moans turn to a chaotic, arrhythmic frenzy of erotic sounds and her body writhes beneath me that I know she's on the edge. I pull my arm off her waist, letting her move however she wants as I palm her tit again with one hand, and with the other, I slip a third finger inside her pussy. She huffs and groans, and I push her further, flicking my tongue over her clit, then sucking it between my lips.

The orgasm explodes through her. Dee screams up at the ceiling as she grinds against my fingers, riding the waves. I savor her ecstasy almost as much as she does, delighting in the sight of her wild eyes watching me bring on another wave.

My cock is painfully hard, again, a fucking beast begging to join the party. I need her, all of her, right now, again and again and always. I crawl up her body, shoving her shirt up to her neck so I can suck and nibble on her pert nipples as I keep finger fucking her. Finally when my mouth is at her jaw, near her ear, I tell her, "I need you to come on my cock now, baby."

She answers in a whisper. "Yes."

Fuck yes.

I pull my fingers out of her pussy, slipping them into my mouth for another taste before I grab the condom from my pocket and sheath up. Then, with a sharp thrust, I fill her. She arches her back, her tits pressing up against my chest as her tight little pussy squeezes around me. Groaning, I freeze, barely hanging on, like I'm a teenager, and this is our first time…again. But in a way, it is like the first time all over again, a new beginning. And it feels so good, too good.

When I wrest some control back from my teenaged libido, I start to move inside her, and it's amazing. The feel of her, so soft and warm and tight, so perfect. She was always so perfect for me, the perfect fit in every way. How was I so stupid to forget that, to forget us? Dee looks up at me with a curious expression, almost like she's surprised to find it's me here, too, surprised that it's *us* tangled together on her couch.

Then, she kisses me. Unlike the other kisses we've shared lately, there's no anger in this one, no biting rage. Dee kisses me like she used to, with all the heart and soul I used to love, I *still* love. I slow my pace, kissing her with long smooth slips of my tongue as I slide my cock deeper in a steady rhythm.

It's like we've forgotten ourselves, our history, our pain. Like this perfect moment is tabula rasa, a blank slate where we can start again, write a new history together. Or at least I hope that's what it is I'm feeling because right now, in her arms, in her body, it's all I want.

That thought alone nearly brings me to orgasm, but not yet, not before Dee. I focus every ounce of energy on her, listening for her cues, her tells, remembering, relearning what works. And soon, she's gasping, little beads of sweat dotting her forehead and dampening the hair around her face as she moves with me. We build and build together, until she tenses beneath me, all around me, her arms hugging my neck, her thighs around my waist, and she cries out with pleasure. She's so beautiful like this. She's always beautiful, but right now she's vulnerable too. I can see her completely for the first time since I came back. And, God, I've missed her.

I come, tensing all over and groaning as I press deep inside her and feel everything, overwhelmingly, in that moment. Then every muscle in my body quits, turns to jelly. I roll to my side to keep from crushing her, pulling her with me until she's wrapped in my arms.

My breath tickles the stray strands of hair that fan out from her forehead, and her breath tickles my chest. It feels like heaven.

I open my mouth to tell her, to declare the truth, that I love her more now, in this moment, than in any moment before. But she speaks first. "You may leave now."

I freeze, not sure what she means. "You're granting me permission to go?"

"No," she sits up, awkwardly detangling our arms and legs, and tugs her shirt back down over her breasts, "I'm telling you to go."

Still sprawled across her couch, condom still on my cock, I watch her hobble to the crumple of fabric on the floor. She moves to sit in a chair opposite me so she can slip her underwear back on.

"What was this?" I ask as I sit up then stand and tug my jeans back into place, zipping them up one-handed as I look for a trash can for the used condom.

She points toward the kitchen, where I find the trash and toss the rubber, groaning when she replies, "We already talked about this. You agreed. It's just fucking."

Back in the living room, I try not to look too mad as I tug my T-shirt back on. "And nothing more?"

"Nothing more." She nods, but she won't look me in the eyes when she says it.

I give that some thought, finally declaring, "Bullshit."

"Just go," she huffs and hobbles away from me, collecting her crutches and then swinging her way to the kitchen to grab a beer from her fridge. She doesn't offer me one, but why would she if she's trying to get me to leave?

I glance around her apartment, really seeing it now for the first time. It's simple, uncluttered, practical. Not a lot of photos dot the walls, just a couple shots of her with her fire station crew, one of her receiving an award from the mayor. No family pictures, no images of friends outside of work; the space is too quiet, too calm, not like a home, more like a hotel, a bed and a shower for her to use when she's away from her real home at the fire station.

It makes me sad, and it makes me angry…at myself. All our lives, Dee was a loner. With no siblings and addict parents, she was used to being alone. Then, for some strange reason, she decided to trust me enough to let me into her life. When her mom overdosed a few years later, she turned even further inward, building steep walls around herself. And I was the only person she let inside.

Then I walked away. I went to war and left her behind. I won't do that again. Not ever. She wants me to leave right now, and okay, of course I'll do as she asks, but not before saying, "I know you still care about me. I saw it in your eyes. I *felt* it in your—"

"So what if I do? It doesn't change anything."

"It changes everything."

"How?" She frowns at me, crossing her arms awkwardly over her crutches.

"We can…I don't know…*fix* this."

"Fix what?"

"Us!"

"There is no *us*, Rico." She still she won't meet my eyes. She's lying, and she knows I know she's lying.

I've been able to detect her bullshit since we were eight years old. What makes this so interesting is that I know she knows I know she's lying. Oddly enough, I consider this progress. I'll cut my losses, for now. "Can we fuck again, at least?"

Now she looks at me, and there's a spark there, that little twinkle of something good. She chews on her bottom lip and picks at her freckle before finally saying, "I'll think about it."

Sounds like yes to me.

"Wipe that stupid grin off your face before I change my answer to 'hell no!' "

"Yes, ma'am," I say as I go to her, kiss her on the cheek, then head for the door. "I'll see you soon."

"Not if you keep calling me ma'am." Dee gets in the last word, and I let her have it, whistling as I head down to my car.

"Did you have a good day, mijo?" mamá asks as I come into the kitchen.

"Yeah. Just dropped in to see how Dee's doing." I join Matty at the table where he's coloring. I pick him up for a hug, then sit in his chair, and place him on my lap. With a kiss to the top of his head, I steal a crayon and start coloring. "How was church, buddy?"

"It was awesome! We colored."

I'm just now noticing we're coloring a picture of a shepherd and lamb.

Now Matty leans in, his eyes wide as he whispers loudly, "And I got to drink wine!"

"Oh you did, did you?" I ask my son, while behind him mamá shakes her head, trying not to laugh. I'm pretty sure Father Paul pours juice for communion, not wine, but I let Matty enjoy his big-kid moment. "Did you like it?"

Matty sort of shrugs, entirely focused on coloring again.

"How is Dee?" mamá sets a plate of food in front of me. Food is her love language. It's nice, but I'm going to gain twenty pounds living with her again.

"She's good." I try to act casual—like I'm not remembering the feel of her, the taste of her—while I talk to my mother and my son. "She could probably use some more food though. I'm sure it's hard for her to shop in that cast."

Dee's going to kill me for sending mamá over with food, but at least it will give her a reason to reach out and yell at me.

"Or, you could cook dinner for her again," mamá suggests. I glance up from my plate of mole to see her grinning at me. "I'm sure Matty would love another evening playing with the cats."

Matty squeals with joy. "When? When?"

Cornered, I look between them both. "We'll see."

At that, mamá winks at me.

Damn. I'm pretty sure she knows what I got up to with Dee this afternoon. And I think she's encouraging me to get up to it again.

I breathe it in, that smell of the station. Though really, it's just the smell of coffee, some fancy flavor Watts likes to bring in. The man loves his coffee, and I've missed that about him. I've missed so much; like the sound of the weights clanking and the washing machine whirring and the guys in the kitchen cooking lunch. I've missed the energy of our comradery at the station and the sharp focus we share when we ride out together. I've missed it all.

It's pathetic to admit, but this is my home. Just a day into my medical leave, that reality hit me hard: my apartment is where I sleep between shifts, but this is where I *live*. The fire service has been my whole life, for my entire adult life. On the days when I'm not on shift, I'm volunteering for all the overtime they'll give me because this is what I love. And it's all I have.

Normal people have lives, don't they? Families and friends? For me, these guys are my life, my family, and my best friends. It's a depressing admission, I guess, and one I couldn't ignore or deny as I sat at home, alone, recovering from my injury.

I had to beg Watts to put me back in rotation, even if it's just light duty. I'd have done anything to get away from that lonely sad place, where all I had to do each day was think. Thank God, I'm here, back in my happy place, where I can deny the heavy truth of my empty life, at least for the next twenty-four hours.

"I heard you have another date tomorrow night." Rooster elbows me in the side as I walk into the apparatus bay. Now that I'm in a boot and don't need the crutches, he's making up for lost elbow time. Apparently.

I glare at him. "It's not a date. It's dinner."

"Exactly what do you think a *date* is, if not dinner—?"

"And it's not *another* date seeing as how we never had a *first* date." Except, we did have a first date, way back when we were sixteen. And, yeah, I guess having dinner alone at a man's home could be construed as a *date*. Some might even consider that rendezvous last week when Rico made my pussy purr like a contented cat a *date* as well. But I will admit to nothing, instead changing the subject. "Don't be such a clucking hen, Rooster."

With that, Rooster waggles his brows as he opens the door to the firehouse kitchen and lounge, and a whole chorus of "surprise!" rings through the air.

"Oh my God, you guys!" I'm truly surprised and touched. My guys —plus the crew from B Shift who are lingering past noon—have thrown me a party with balloons and streamers and a banner that reads, "Welcome Home." I pause a little at the awkward accuracy of being welcomed *home* here, then turn my focus to the cake.

Someone went to Cathy's Cakes over on Pecan Street with instructions for a purple cake with a frosted portrait of a cartoonishly klutzy blond, barely balancing on a pair of crutches, in turnout gear.

It's ridiculous, and I love it. I let out a big belly laugh, probably my first since the Stonehaven fire, and try to hide the fact that they've brought tears to my eyes. There's a round of hugs. Drew grabs a massive knife from the drawer and starts hacking the cake into huge hunks of sugar that Rooster distributes.

The cake has turned Drew's tongue purple when he asks, "So I hear Matty's coming over to hang out with the cats again tomorrow evening. Guess that means you've got another date with the daddy."

Date with the daddy? I groan.

Naively, when I'd invited Rico in, I'd thought I could fuck him *out* of my system. Instead, he's firmly impregnated himself *in* my system. What a dick! Literally. He gives good dick. It's been nothing but Rico, Rico, Rico on the brain and in my dreams for the last week.

When he called and invited me over for dinner tomorrow night, I'm embarrassed to admit how quickly I said yes. Didn't even try to make him work at it. And now that the whole station knows, it's going to be a long shift of this hazing and an even longer shift of wondering what's going to happen when I ring Rico's bell.

Rooster winks at me like he's reading my mind and says, "Cluck! Cluck!"

This time, I don't arrive early. I'd intended to arrive a little late, but I'm an impatient person and couldn't wait around, so here I am on Inez Rodriguez's doorstep, exactly on time.

Rico swings the door open, and he's fucking shirtless, his dog tags looking so goddamn sexy against the rigid bronzed muscles of his chest. He's barefoot, too, wearing only a pair of relaxed jeans that hang enticingly low on his hips. My mouth waters at the sight of him.

Without a word, he steps right out the door and right into my space, wrapping his arms around my waist and lifting me up. He carries me backward, into the house, and kicks the door closed behind us.

Now I see why he texted me earlier to "confirm consent." There's no room for words and negotiations as he takes my mouth in one of those long, languid kisses he's so good at and walks blindly through his childhood home, carrying me past the kitchen to the hall that leads to the bedrooms.

He's a fantastic kisser. With a tongue made of magic, he has my pussy purring within ten seconds of entering his mom's house.

That's talent.

When he finally sets me down, it's on his old bed in his old bedroom, which is full of familiar things. Trophies and medals from high school baseball and track and field clutter the shelves beside stacks of tattered sci-fi novels. And beneath me is Rico's faded blue comforter.

Déjà vu. So many memories of us in this room, studying and doing homework and making out when no one was looking.

Rico reaches for the hem of my shirt and pulls it over my head, then falls to his knees to give my breasts some tender loving care with his hot mouth. Kissing his way down my stomach, he unbuttons my pants and tugs at them. I lift my hips so he can get them down my thighs. He has to take care when tugging them over my boot, but soon enough he's tossing them across the room, and I lie naked on his bed.

I watch as he strips off his own jeans too. But before I've seen my fill, he comes down on me, with his face between my legs, and I yelp as his tongue teases my clit, his hands fisting my hips in a bruising grip.

"I thought you were going to make me dinner, not make me *your* dinner," I joke.

Rico looks up at me from between my thighs, then rises and crawls over my body, his weight on his elbows and knees as he hovers over me. He tangles his fingers in my hair so I'm forced to stare deep into those dark eyes. "First, I'll feed you my cock. Then I'll make you dinner."

Well. Shit. That sounds like a really good plan. And if he keeps talking like that, I'm going to make a wet spot on this blue comforter without him ever having to touch me.

But he does keep touching me. With a squeeze of his fist in my hair, he pulls my head back and the sharp little tug on my scalp hurts so good. I moan, and he drowns me in another of his deep kisses.

I adored Rico when he was a boy, but he's so damn sexy as a man. He makes me desperate for him, ravenous. I run my hands down the tight muscles of his chest and abdomen and palm his thick, veiny length, teasing him like he's teasing me.

With a growl in my ear, he says, "There's a condom on the nightstand. Put it on me."

Despite the order, he barely gives me any room to work, his weight hovering just inches above me. Caged beneath him, I manage to find the condom, tear open the wrapper, and roll it down his cock. With that done, I look up to meet his gaze and spread my legs wider. It's all the invitation he needs, and he shifts his hips forward to take me with one sharp thrust.

Ah. Fuck. It hurts a little. It hurts so good.

The last time we were together, he made love to me. This time, he fucks me, hard and fast and so fucking well. Hands still tangled in my hair, he pulls my head back so he can nip and bite my neck, his hot breath scolding my skin as he pistons his hips in a punishing rhythm. It's so sexy, this animal inside him, this desperation coming out. Everything about him does me in, always has, but the way he fucks me right now—it ruins me so exquisitely.

I'm going to come. Heat starts low in my belly and grows and grows and grows, consuming me with fire. All my muscles tense, seizing and wrapping tighter around him. My legs twist around his hips. My arms choke his neck as I hang on. All it takes is one low, sexy grunt from him, that sound of his desire, his desperation hot against my ear, and the orgasm explodes through me. I scream from the intensity of it as my body, my mind, my heart, and my soul—all of me— comes undone.

Rico comes, too, his breath fluttering the hair by my ear as he lets go.

Holy shit.

I shiver beneath him like I'm cold. I'm not cold. Still, Rico rolls to the side of me and grabs the edge of the blue comforter to bring over me, wrapping his arms around me so I'm cradled against him, enveloped in his heat.

It's bliss, this place where I've found myself. Back in Rico's embrace after all this time. There's still a part of me that doesn't trust him, doesn't trust myself with him, but right now, that part rests while the other part of me, the part that perks up with excitement every time he's near, comes out to play.

"Weird," he says.

"What's weird?"

He doesn't answer for a moment, like he's considering, then he says cryptically, "I feel strange."

Strange is a strange way to phrase it, but I feel it too. Everything about this is strange and—

"My head is killing me, and I can't focus my eyes."

"What?" I frown at him. He's looking right at me but blinking his eyes like he's trying to clear his vision. I sit up, and he doesn't move with me, still blinking his eyes and rubbing his forehead.

I flick on the bedside lamp, and Rico flinches, his speech sounding slurred as he mumbles, "That hurts."

"What hurts?" I need him to clarify.

"Head."

"Describe the pain."

"Painful," he says, and I roll my eyes. But then he elaborates, "It moves."

"Moves?"

"Everywhere, like lightning. Flashes. I feel it behind my teeth right now, no, my temples. Back of head."

Shit. I jump up from the bed and reach for my pants, digging my phone out of the back pocket. "And your vision is blurred?"

"Yeah."

"One eye or both?"

He furrows his brow but then starts alternating one eye open and one eye closed. "Mostly my left eye. Can't focus. All blurry."

"Shit," I mutter as I dial Drew's number.

"What are you...why...you... I can't..." Rico is staring at me with that unfocused gaze, not making any sense.

Drew picks up on the second ring. "Hey, what's up?"

"I need you to come over here, but I don't want to alarm Mateo. Can Chloe watch him for a little bit while you help me?"

"Yeah, sure. Help you with what?"

I glance over at Rico, who's trying to sit up in his bed but struggles to get upright. To Drew, I say, "Rico is having a stroke."

"What?" I frown at Dee. Did she say *stroke*? I… That wouldn't… doesn't…no sense.

I blink again, trying to focus my eyes. Everything is blurry, like before I got LASIK, when I'd take my contacts out. But unlike then, blinking and rubbing my eyes doesn't help.

And my head. The pain. It started as a dull ache. Now it's sharp, electric, zapping around. It hits my skull, moving from one side to the other, pierces my forehead, slices down my neck. I hold my hands to my eyes, my temples, like applying pressure will help. It doesn't.

Trying to sit up, I fail. My left arm isn't doing its job; it moves like it's asleep, heavy and uncoordinated, a weight at my side. Like my hand isn't attached to my brain anymore. It's not receiving the command for what to do, and so it's not doing it. *Close fingers*, I think to my left hand. My fingers twitch a little, move slightly, but don't close. My right hand does better; I close those fingers. Still a struggle though.

Dee rushes over to me. She's dressed now. When did that happen? She pushes me onto my back and slides a pair of my athletic shorts up my legs. Where did she find them? The drawer or the hamper? Am I clean or dirty? She pulls the condom off my dick and tosses it into the trash can under my old desk.

Dirty. Definitely dirty.

There's banging, a knocking noise from somewhere. Dee vanishes. Closing my eyes, I pinch the bridge of my nose to try and relieve the new pain that's landed there.

"—experiencing head pain, blurred vision, and aphasia," Dee says as she returns to the room.

I open my eyes as Drew walks through my bedroom doorway, and I quickly look down to check that Dee tucked my cock away. Shorts are on. Yep. When I open my mouth to say something to Drew and Dee, the words that come out are, "What's aphasia?"

They ignore my question, and Drew kneels beside the bed so we're eye level. "Hey, man. I'm gonna check a couple things. Can you sit up?"

I try. Can't. Drew helps, and I'm upright, sort of slumped against the wall, staring at him but not really seeing him. He flashes a light in my eyes, and I flinch. He puts a cuff around my arm that gets tighter and tighter, like it's going to cut off my arm above the elbow before the pressure finally lets up.

"Swallow for me," Drew instructs.

Odd request, but I do it. He nods.

"Okay, let's get you to the hospital," Drew says as he slots himself under one of my arms. Dee gets under the other.

I try to point out that she's in a cast and shouldn't be putting my weight on her bum ankle, but my words don't work, and she seems to be managing okay. With their help, I barely have to walk, which is good because my feet aren't responding correctly to my commands. And it feels like my toes are tangled in the carpet. Even though… Wait… I look down at the tile floor. Mamá doesn't have carpet in the hallway. What am I tangled in?

Outside, they lead me past my car and Dee's car to a big, black truck parked in the drive. The engine is running, its headlights shine in our eyes as we approach, and the driver's side door hangs wide open, like Drew just threw it in park and ran to the house.

They work efficiently together, getting me into the back seat like I'm the patient on one of their emergency calls. Except Dee slides into the back seat beside me and slips her hand into mine, lacing our fingers together. That's probably not standard operating procedure. And I like it. I fixate on it. Until Drew slams a door shut and jolts me out of my thoughts.

Suddenly, we're moving. Too fast. Too much motion. Too much… everything. Headlights of oncoming cars spike through the windshield. I flinch as panic rushes through me, certain the cars are about to hit us head on. But impact never comes as they harmlessly pass us by. I avert my eyes from the windshield to the dashboard, where the yellow hazard-lights indicator is blinking. It's too-perfect rhythm taps against my forehead. I close my eyes, but that makes me feel nauseated. So I look down at my lap, staring at Dee's hand in mine, and focus on breathing.

Dee's voice sounds from my side. Too loud. Too sharp. Too much. While normally I love the sound of her voice, right now it hurts, like she's yelling into my ear. "Janis, we have a Level 1 STROKE ALERT en route. ETA is—"

"Three minutes," Drew hollers from the driver's seat. His voice hurts too.

"Three minutes," Dee repeats into the phone. "Patient's name is Ricardo Rodriguez, Hispanic male, age twenty-nine, weight—" She glances at me, like she's expecting me to fill in the blank.

I know my weight, I see the numbers in my mind, but I can't grab them with my mouth to spit them out.

Dee frowns at me and looks away, continuing, "About one hundred eighty-five pounds, suffering from confusion with aphasia, partial numbness left side, visual complaints, and severe headache."

I don't listen to much more of what Dee says; my attention is fixed back on the road and the way Drew drives it. It's like we're hurdling through space, too fast. He doesn't stop at red lights, only pauses before speeding forward. I flinch and flinch again. I want to tell him to slow down, but I can't get to those words.

It's like there's a deep gorge in my brain, and the words I need are on the other side, and the rope bridge connecting the two sides is falling apart and unstable—

"Red," I say, so relieved I found the word and got it out of me. And I manage to elaborate for clarity. "Red light."

"We're almost there, baby," Dee says.

I'm struck by how sweet her voice sounds, how soft her words feel. She doesn't talk to me like she talked to the person on the phone, and I like this tone so much better. Plus, she called me "baby," and that feels like heaven. Which is a strange feeling right now because I think I might be dying.

And if I am dying, I have some things I need to say. "I didn't get to feed you."

That's not what I was going to say.

Dee raises a brow, looking a little confused and a little wicked. She squeezes my hand again. "You filled me up just fine."

From the front seat, Drew mumbles, "TMI."

I turn to Dee and look at her, wishing I could see her better. "I never stopped loving you. I never will. You and Matty, you're my whole heart. I screwed up so badly, and I'm so sorry, and I miss you, and if I die—"

Dee grabs my face, bringing my gaze right to hers, forcing me to see her as she says, "You're not dying. You're having a stroke, yes, but if it was going to kill you, you'd be dead already."

A comforting thought.

"We're getting you to the hospital as quickly as we can so they can administer a medication that can reverse some or all of your symptoms."

"Oh." I'd hoped for something else from her in this moment, but that's good news too.

Drew whips the car into the hospital parking lot, and I slide across the seat a little as he loops in under the ambulance portico. There's a whole crowd of people in lab coats and scrubs, standing around an empty gurney, waiting.

As soon as Drew hits the brakes and slides the gear into park, he and Dee jump out of the truck, and all those waiting people spring into action. I'm helped from the truck to the stretcher. Once I'm horizontal, with Dee standing beside me, her fingers once again laced with mine, she yells at Drew, "Find Inez. She's at church, at the cathedral."

"On it." Drew nods and jumps back in his truck. Within a matter of moments, he's out of the parking lot, his flashers still blinking in the inky blackness of the night.

We're on the move, too, my vertigo making me feel sick again as I'm shoved down some corridor where the ceiling lights hit at regular intervals, like a strobe. I close my eyes and flop a listless arm over my face, even as someone is talking to me, asking me something.

"No known allergies. Right, Rico?" Dee says as she hurries along beside me, still holding my hand, grounding me.

I squeeze her hand and mumble. "Yes."

"That's yes, you have allergies. Or yes, no known allergies?" some other woman asks.

I look to Dee, and she answers for me. "He has no known allergies."

The rolling comes to a stop, and I slip my arm off my eyes to take a peek. We've arrived in a room now, and I'm surrounded by people, all flitting around like fireflies.

Someone takes my hand and says something to me just before she pricks one of my fingers. Someone else wraps a monitoring device around a different finger and a blood pressure cuff around one of my arms. I flinch as someone temporarily blinds both eyes with a penlight, exacerbating my headache.

There's another prick, this time in my left elbow. And then yet another prick in my right elbow. I frown, this one hurting more than all the rest, and look down at my arms, like I'll find a pack of Dracula's brides there, sucking the life out of me. But it's just IVs, two of them, one in each arm.

Why two? I want to ask someone, but the medical team operates like a pit crew at the Indianapolis 500, where every second counts. I don't want to interrupt.

Like with Drew, I'm asked to swallow. But now they also want me to hold up each of my legs and arms. It all strikes me as a bit odd, but I do as commanded.

"Good," the nurse says. "Now, I need to take your jewelry off before we take you for a scan, okay?"

Jewelry? What jewelry?

Before I can get clarity, she reaches for my dog tags and goes to lift them over my head. Oh. Those. I've worn them since basic training. They aren't *jewelry* to me; they're my identity. I watch the nurse hand my identity to Dee for safekeeping. I'm comfortable with that, so I don't lodge a complaint.

Once I'm stripped of my ID, the nurse fits a nasal cannula into my nostrils. The oxygen smells strange, but I breathe it anyway. Another nurse clips a plastic bracelet on me. It's my new identity: from fighter to patient in under ten seconds.

"Okay, let's get a scan of your brain, see what's going on in there," one of the nurses says, and they start to push my bed toward the door again.

Wait. I grab for Dee, clutching her hand. I'm overwhelmed and at a loss for words, but what I have to say is vitally important: "No MRI."

Those are the only words I can reach, like all my other words are stuck to the roof of my mouth. So I move my hand to my bum shoulder, the one with the remnants of shrapnel embedded in it.

And God bless her, Dee understands. She's always been able to understand me, sometimes better than I understand myself. "Shrapnel from the war?"

I nod.

"It's okay." She squeezes my hand, and I feel my dog tags in her palm, warm from her grip. "This is a CT scan, nonmagnetic, so you'll be fine."

I grin a bit, relieved she understands and exhausted from the exertion to communicate. The staff start pushing my bed again. Dee stands still, letting my hand go as the distance grows between us.

"Don't leave me," I beg, desperate to hold onto her.

"I'll be right here, Rico. They'll bring you back after your scan. I'm not going anywhere."

I'm not going anywhere. Those words are a comfort I didn't know I needed.

A frisson of fear creeps down my spine like the legs of a thousand spiders, leaving me shivering and breathless as the nurses wheel Rico toward the CT suite. I haven't felt this kind of fear since I came home from school one day and found Mom nonresponsive on the bathroom floor.

That was the day I lost her. Though, the loss of Mom was a slow one. I'd been losing her in small doses for weeks, months, years before that final, toxic goodbye.

At least this time I'd known what to do. With Drew's help, we'd gotten Rico the medical care he needed very fast. I just hope—for the sake of Rico, Inez, and Mateo—that it was fast enough.

Oh, who am I kidding? I hold out hope for myself too. As much as I like to kid myself that I can have an affair with Rico that's purely physical, it's a shallow little lie, and we both know it. *Everyone* knows it.

Rico stole my heart when we were eight, and he never gave it back. Since he left me, no one else has come close to mattering as much as Rico did. Not sexually, or otherwise. He was my best friend before he was my one great love, and for a long time, I've had neither of those things. When Rico left, he took my heart with him.

I tried to move on. I worked to fit the pieces of my shattered heart back together while the world kept turning, indifferent. But it was too much work. Too much struggle. I got lazy, and then I became indifferent too. Indifference can be pretty fun, actually. I partied like I didn't care because caring hurt too much. Dad called me a heartbreaker for the way I "dated" the men of South Central Texas, but how can you break a heart you never even touched?

I was indifferent in other ways, too, not bothering much with friendships. Rooster is probably the closest friend I have now, but he has four big sisters and doting parents. If he landed himself in the hospital, I wouldn't be in his top five list of people to call first. I love Drew like a brother, too, but he has Chloe now. He's never going to need much from a friend like me when he has the love of his life to depend on. And Watts: he's a family man, in a whole other world from the lonely one in which I live.

That's the heart of it, really: I'm alone. And I've been alone for a long time. If I landed my ass in the hospital, who would I call?

Oh right, I did land my ass in the hospital. I look down at the boot on my foot and remember waking up to see Rico there, asleep in the chair across from me. And in that moment, for the first time in a long time, I didn't feel alone.

With a groan, I flop into one of the chairs in Rico's room, humming the chorus of an old Joan Jett song to calm my nerves as I wait for his return.

My hand hurts. I look down to see I'm still clutching his dog tags, my grip so tight the edges have left marks in my palm. Relaxing my fingers, I open my hand to read the details stamped into the metal, tracing my thumb over the indentations that spell out Rico's name, social security number, blood type, and religion.

I remember, when he enlisted, he'd stewed about what to declare as his religion. Rico's not religious—always a questioner, never a believer —but his mother would have disowned him if he'd listed anything other than Catholic on his ID.

It still reads Catholic, and I wonder if these are the same tags he wore all those years ago when he kissed me goodbye? How long has this pair hung against his chest, over his heart, only to come off now, as he lies in a hospital.

I'm shaken from my thoughts when Inez rushes into the room and pulls me out of my chair, entangling me in a tight hug. This tiny woman is deceptively strong. I take comfort in her embrace, letting some of the tension drain out of me as I set my chin on her shoulder and glance over at Drew, standing in the doorway. I give him a thumbs-up as thanks for bringing her here.

"How is he?" Inez pulls away so she can look me in the eyes as I answer.

I encourage her to sit in one of the available chairs, and I sit in the other. "His medical team performed what's called an NIHSS assessment to determine the severity of his stroke. He scored a six, which is in the mild to moderately severe range.

"They took him to the CT suite within ten minutes of arrival and are presently performing a scan of his brain. The medical team says he's a good candidate for Tenecteplase, which is a relatively new thrombolytic agent used to treat acute ischemic strokes."

The look of confusion on Inez's face suggests I need to explain better, in layman's terms.

"It can dissolve the clot in his brain and stop it from causing any more damage. Oftentimes, it can even reverse the effect of the stroke and relieve symptoms. Rico's symptoms are relatively mild: some numbness on his left side, difficulty speaking, trouble focusing his vision, and a severe headache."

Inez looks terrified. I need to stop talking. But I add, "He's in good hands, Inez. He's going to be okay."

"Thank you for being there for him." Inez reaches across to hold my hand, her grip squeezing Rico's dog tags tighter into my palm.

I don't know what to say, and it's not like I could get any words around the lump in my throat anyway. When Inez releases my hand, I stare at Rico's tags and clear my throat. "Do you want his—?"

Inez pats my palm. "No, Dee Marie, you hold onto those for him."

Still hovering in the doorway, Drew asks, "Inez, should I bring Mateo here?"

We both turn our attention to him as Inez considers.

Sensing her hesitation, Drew quickly offers, "Or he can have a slumber party with the cats tonight."

Inez's expression lightens. "You wouldn't mind? I know it is a lot to ask—"

"Nonsense. He's a good kid, and the cats love all the attention he gives them. We'd be happy to host him for a cat slumber party." Drew crosses the room and hugs Inez, his big arms completely cocooning her.

When he wraps those big arms around me next, I take a deep breath and let some of my tension go. Quietly, he assures me, "He'll be okay."

I don't know why I needed to hear that so much, but I did. As a firefighter—and a trained EMT—I know we got him here quickly, and the hospital is treating him in a thorough and timely manner, all important in the case of a stroke. But I think I needed someone else to say those words—*he'll be okay*—before I could truly believe them.

"All right. I'm heading back to the house. You both have my number. Call when you have news or want me to bring Mateo here in the morning." Drew backs out of the doorway, and then it's just Inez and me in the patient room, which feels too large without the patient in it.

I glance over at Inez. She looks terrified, her posture rigid, her knuckles strained where she's squeezing her purse tightly. I reach over, trying to coax her to relax her grip.

Using Drew's comforting words, I say, "He's going to be okay."

She forces a grin at me, like she appreciates the effort, but she tells me, "His father died of a stroke."

"Oh." *How had I forgotten about that?*

"He was only fifty. I've been worried about my boys ever since. But I never thought it would be Ricky…"

She drifts off, and a heavy pall of silence fills the room. I should say something more, comfort her, but I'm too stunned as I remember when Rico got the news of his father's death. They'd called him out of class that day, and then he didn't come back. I'd ridden my bike all the way over to his house, then beyond it up the hill to our tree. I'd found him there, trying not to cry.

"Do they know what caused Manny Senior's stroke?"

Inez looks at me and shakes her head.

I don't want to pry, but I'm not sure what to say next. I know she's worried, but telling her that stroke treatments have improved significantly in the years since her husband's death feels like the wrong thing to say right now. I think what we both need is the quiet.

We don't get it. There's a clamor at the door, heralding Rico's return. I stand from my chair at the same time Inez stands from hers, both of us angling for a view of him, some glimpse to give us hope that our Rico is okay.

When he sees us there and smiles a little, that's when it hits me like a mallet to the head: *Goddammit! I fucking love Rico. I always have. I always will.*

His first words upon seeing us both are, "Where's Matty? Is he okay?"

And wouldn't you know, that just makes me fall more in love with him.

"He's going to have a cat slumber party at Drew and Chloe's house tonight," I tell him.

Rico slowly nods, seeming to relax a little.

Inez goes to his side, touching his face like he's still her baby boy, sick in bed. She clutches his hand to her chest and asks. "¿Mijo, estás bien?"

"Si, mamá, estoy bien."

They're empty words; we all know it. There is nothing "okay" about having a stroke, but I think hearing Rico's voice is a comfort to Inez. The words hardly matter; it's that he's speaking—without slurring or stuttering—which is important.

Rico reaches his free hand toward me, and I come up beside Inez to take it. His grip is stronger than before, his gaze more focused. It's clear they've already administered the treatment meds, and the meds are working.

With a wink at me, Rico tells Inez, "Dee saved my life, mamá."

"You weren't going to die." I smirk, playing down the drama.

"She saved me," he insists. "I didn't know what was happening to me, but she did. She and Drew raced me here."

The attention on me makes me itchy. I squirm and shuffle from foot to foot. "I can identify most rashes too. That one's a real party pleaser."

Inez smiles at me, her face sweet and tearstained. She wraps an arm around my waist and pulls me closer. It feels like she's pulling me into their family, adopting me as one of her pack, just like old times.

A doctor with salt-and-pepper hair and a starched white lab coat comes into the room. His name is stitched on his breast pocket, Dr. Thomas, but he introduces himself, then says, "Okay, so as I told Mr. Rodriguez, we believe he's having an acute stroke. Because you got him to the hospital within four and a half hours of the time when he was last known well, there is a treatment that we administered to him, with his permission, in the CT suite. It's a powerful clot-busting medicine called Tenecteplase. There is a small chance he could develop bleeding in his brain. But it's the best option we have for restoring blood flow to the brain." He pauses, as if leaving room for questions. When none come right away, he continues, "Rico, get comfortable because you're going to be here a while. You will be under close monitoring for the next twenty-four hours. Then tomorrow, we'll do another CT scan to see how things are going. Sound like a plan?"

It's a rhetorical question, but we all nod anyway.

Dr. Thomas claps his hands together. "Great. You've got Bailey as your dedicated nurse for the next several hours. Ring her if you need anything or feel any new or unusual sensations. I'll be back to check on you in the morning."

Once the doctor leaves, we're all frozen for a moment, a little shell-shocked. It's a lot of information to take in. Rico had a stroke...while we were having sex.

Jesus, I could have killed the love of my life with my pussy!

"Where's Matty?" Rico asks.

His mom and I both glance at him, concerned. Didn't we just tell him that? Professionally, I know memory issues are common with a stroke. But witnessing it happen with Rico is...difficult.

As calmly as I can, I repeat myself. "He's at Drew and Chloe's house. They're going to have a cat slumber party tonight. They'll bring him in the morning when you're feeling better."

Rico's brows knit together. "You already told me that didn't you?"

I smile, and his mom squeezes his hand. I look at my own hands and open the fist that still clutches Rico's dog tags.

"Here are these back," I say when I set them gently on his chest.

My hand is too empty without them in my grasp. Which doesn't make sense. Why would I hold any sentiment for the symbol of the life he lived without me?

"I forget sometimes that I even wear them. Habit. I guess." Rico touches them, flipping one over and reading them both. "Mamá, do you want to keep them?"

Inez frowns as she looks between us. "But, they're your identity."

Rico holds up his wrist, where the plastic hospital wristband hangs askew. "I have new ID now." He grins at his mom before adding, "And I'm not the guy who needs those, not anymore. But I know you like to hang onto things, so you keep them."

Inez nods as she pinches her lips between her teeth like she's fighting the urge to cry and slips the tags into her purse. Watching this shared moment between mother and son makes me feel uneasy, like I'm invading some sacred space where I don't belong.

Taking a step toward the door, I try not to interrupt too much as I say, "I should go, let you two—"

"No." Rico practically shouts and tries to sit up, but all the cords and wires tie him down to the bed. "Please don't leave me, Dee. *Please.*"

I blink at him, stunned. What a thing to say.

Rico reaches for me, and I clasp his fingers with mine. The grip in his left hand is a little weaker than normal, so I squeeze harder, like maybe I can strengthen this connection between us from my end.

The door opens with a jolt, and I nearly jump out of my skin as Rico's nurse comes in for his first fifteen-minute check. All thoughts of leaving are gone now. I pull up a chair beside Inez and stay.

CHAPTER 16
RICO

Sleep is impossible when they're checking on me minute to minute and then hour to hour. As soon as I drift off, they wake me again, performing tests to determine if my stroke symptoms are improving. They are. The partial blindness seems to be gone; the headache is gone too. The numbness on my left side has reduced to lingering tingles in my fingers and toes. The brain fog has mostly lifted, which is the biggest relief, though I still struggle with memory and recall.

The doctor says I'm lucky. All I feel is tired. Everything. Every damn thing is exhausting right now.

Getting up to take a piss a few hours ago was like a high school production of Shakespeare: awkward. I need to pee again, and the nurse brought me a little jug she called a "portable urinal" so I don't have to get up again. I can just pee right here in front of everyone.

Yeah, no. I'll hold it.

Mamá and Dee are finally asleep, each of them stretched out in one of the lounge chairs in my room. The chairs dwarf my mom, her feet barely touching the floor. And they're too small for Dee, whose long legs stretch out in front of her. Having slept in one of those chairs when I'd sat in Dee's hospital room a few weeks ago, I know from experience there's no Goldilocks chair here.

There's nothing to do but watch television. Normally, this would bore me, but tonight, as tired as I am, I just stare at the moving colors and faces. When there's text on the screen, I struggle to read it. I can see the words—my vision is better now—but my brain can't easily associate those words with what they represent.

I'm told *this* is what aphasia is, and so far, it seems to be the most significant lingering effect of the stroke. After staring at the television for a while, I tilt my head toward my mom, then look over at Dee.

I can't stop wondering: Is she here out of obligation, or does she still care?

Obligation, obviously. I begged Dee to stay with me. I didn't give her much choice. So now, she sleeps awkwardly on that uncomfortable chair. Yeah, I'm an asshole for pressuring her to stay. But every time I look at her, I feel better.

Outside, it's first light, the town painted in dusty purples and pinks before the sun crests the horizon and it's all awash in orange. All I can think about as I watch the sun rise is my little man. I miss him. I need to see him.

Dee and mamá were right not to bring him here last night, but the separation is difficult. Last night was the first time we've slept under separate roofs since I gained full custody. And since that day, I've made it a point to always be home for him at bedtime so he knows he's sleeping in a safe, familiar home with a family who cherishes and adores him.

How did he do at Drew and Chloe's house? Is he upset that I'm not there? After his brief stint in foster care, he'd had a few panic attacks and a lot of nightmares to overcome, but we've managed to do so with consistency and routine. He needs stability, not a slumber party at the neighbor's house while his dad is hooked to a bunch of machines in the hospital.

And for my part, I'm as dependent on him as I imagine he is on me. I've wanted to see him so badly; all night I've longed for one of Matty's smiles or even just the quiet peace I see on his face when he sleeps. But it wouldn't have been right to drag him to the hospital at some ungodly hour, when he's tired and I'm a mess. It would have only scared him.

Maybe it's wrong of me to want to have him here with me at all, to witness his big, strong dad in this weakened state. But I've found that when it comes to Matty's peace of mind, honesty is the best policy. So I texted Drew in the middle of the night—one eye closed as I focused on the keys of mamá's phone, trying to remember how to spell the words I needed—asking him to bring Matty once he wakes up.

When I hear the knock at my door, I assume it's the nurse again, here for another wellness check. Then the door opens, and I see Drew and Chloe standing there, Matty between them, and my heart sings. His eyes go wide when he sees me. He looks terrified, and I wish now I'd spoken to him on the phone first, before he had to see me like this.

I smile as best I can. "Hey, buddy, come on in. It's okay."

He comes to my bedside, staring more at his feet than at me, like he's afraid of what I look like. I glance at the mirror over the sink and don't think I look any different. But looking down at my arms, the blood pressure cuff, the dual IVs, the pulse ox clip on my finger, yeah, maybe it's all a little scary.

I try to look extra healthy for him, picking him up and setting him on my lap. The IVs pull a little in at my elbows, but I just smile as I kiss him on the forehead and hug him close to me.

I feel a hundred times better having him here. And when he snuggles against me, resting his head under my chin, it's like my heart explodes. I wonder if the nurses will see that as an anomaly on the monitors. I kiss the top of his head, breathing him in, and close my eyes, truly relaxing for the first time in hours.

After a moment, Matty shifts a little in my arms and plays with his wrist, still fresh out of his cast a few days ago, and asks in a hushed voice, "Daddy, did you get broken too?"

What a loaded question. I grin against the top of his head, then answer as honestly as I know how. "No, I just hurt my head last night. The doctors hooked me up to all these machines so they can see why it hurts and make it feel better."

"Does it hurt now?"

"Nope! I feel much better now."

Matty looks at me, his dark eyes shining with unshed tears.

Quickly, I try to lighten the mood. I turn my head so he can inspect the inside of my ear. "Can you see anything wrong in there?"

He grabs my earlobe and comes in close, his little breath tickling my neck as he peers into the darkness of my ear. When that's done, I turn my head so Doctor Matty can inspect the other one. Once I have the all clear, I give him my most wicked grin, and then I start to tickle him. His laughter is like music to my ears, the cure for what ails me. Just five minutes with him, and I'm a new man. All better.

When his giggles subside, he asks, "When can you come home, Daddy?"

I love that he's already calling mamá's house "home." A home was the one thing I couldn't give him for a while, but finally, here in my old home, he has found his place too. "The doctors need to watch me for a little longer, but I'll be coming home really soon after that. Is that okay with you, buddy?"

He nods, seeming satisfied with all the information I've shared with him so far. Only now does his attention wander to the other people in the room. Drew and Chloe had said they were going to the cafeteria for some food for everyone, leaving Matty and me with Dee and mamá. Matty practically squeals when he finally spots his new best friend sprawled over the too-small chair. "Dee's here!"

"Shh." I coax him to lower his voice. "Let's not wake her and abuela up, okay?"

"Dee's my friend." He tries to whisper, but he's bad at whispering.

I stare at Dee a moment, reminiscing as I tell him, "She's my friend too. Did you know she's been my best friend since I was about your age?"

His eyes go wide with shock. "Really?"

"Really." This is magical news to him, and I love seeing that brightness in his eyes. So I elaborate. "I met her on the playground after I broke my arm. She signed my cast and signed her name so big, she covered up most of the other names. Considering her name just has three letters, I was pretty impressed. That's when I knew she was going to be my best friend for life."

"Is Dee still your best friend?" he asks in that poor attempt at whispering.

"Definitely. Some things never change."

Matty considers for a moment. I always wonder what's going on in his head when he gets quiet like this. I don't remember ever being this thoughtful as a child, but my brilliant little boy's mind is always working.

Finally, he says, "I don't have a best friend for life."

"Well, maybe you just haven't met them yet. Or maybe you have, and you just don't know they're your best friend yet. Maybe your best friend for life signed your cast. Who signed their name the biggest?"

"Cassie, but she's loud."

"Loud?" I have to keep from laughing as my son says this far louder than necessary. "Is that a bad thing?"

He shrugs. "She talks a lot. I don't ever get to talk."

"Well, I'll let you in on a little secret…"

He gives me those big owl eyes again. Matty *loves* secrets.

"Sometimes, it's better to listen."

He seems bored by that nugget of wisdom, so I give him another. "Also, Dee is the loudest person I've ever known, and she never stops talking."

"I'll have you know that I talk the perfect amount at the perfect volume," Dee announces from her chair in the corner, jolting my mom awake. Narrowing those moody green eyes at me, Dee asserts, "And I will hear no arguments to the contrary."

I grin at the room as mamá tries to blink her eyes open, and Dee stretches and yawns.

Excited to see his new best friend is awake—and has been listening to us for a while, apparently—Matty clamors down from my bed and hurries over to Dee.

She scoops him into a hug and sets him on her leg. "Hey, my man, how are you doing?" she asks with a big grin.

"I had a slumber party with the cats!" His words lisp through the gap where another tooth came out last week. It nearly cracks me up, and I wish I had recorded it. I'm going to have to make sure he says it again before his grown-up tooth comes in.

"Well, that sounds super fun. What did you and the cats do?"

"Drew put up a tent in the living room, and he gave me a flashlight so I could tell scary stories to them."

"Oh, yeah, were they scaredy cats?" Dee asks and tickles Matty.

He laughs. Mamá laughs. I laugh. And I fall in love with her again. How many times is this, that I've fallen in love with her in my life? A lot.

I can't believe I was so stupid to leave her. To leave this. This small town had me feeling claustrophobic as a teen, and I'd wanted to get out and see the world. Turns out "the world" is made up of a lot of towns just like this one and a lot of towns that are a whole lot worse. But by the time I learned that, it was too late; the damage was done between Dee and me, and my life had taken a new path. Now, to see those paths intersect in that chair across the room gives me a sense of peace I haven't known in a long time. And peace always makes me nervous.

CHAPTER 17
DEE

Rico falls asleep right in the middle of our conversation. Right in the middle of everything. As Mateo and I chat with Inez, and Drew and Chloe bring food and coffee to share, Rico sleeps.

Clearly, he's exhausted. But healing from a stroke is important work, so we let him rest.

Plus, who would dare wake him when he looks so cute? With his adjustable bed angled up for him to sit, his chin slowly dips toward his chest, and his mouth hangs open a little as he dozes. I need to stop staring at him with my big, dumb, girly grin because Drew is watching me, and he sees too much.

In whispers and gestures, we divvy up tasks. Inez will take Mateo home for lunch and a long nap. Drew's shift starts in an hour, where he'll update Watts and the team about why I'm taking the day off. Chloe will drop into the paper on her way to Austin for classes, let them know about Rico's situation, and give my number to his editor if he wants to talk.

And me? I'm on watch-Rico-sleep duty.

It takes a village, I guess. And I'm the village idiot.

What am I doing here? This is a job for a wife or a caregiver, not a fuck buddy. And yeah, maybe I can acknowledge to myself that I'm feeling something stronger for him, but it's not like we've had that conversation yet. Not that anyone else seems to care. Apparently, this community has already decided Rico and I are more than we've agreed to be, and they're going to make this thing happen come hell or high water. Bunch of no-good busybodies with too much time on their hands.

But really, I should leave. I don't know why I'm still here. Rico's a big boy. He's a grown man who survived a damn war; he doesn't need me watching him sleep like some sparkly vampire.

Still, I stay.

I snooze a little, too, but mostly I stare at this handsome man who was once the boy I loved. I still see him in there, the Rico I used to know. He smiles at me from behind those sad, sexy eyes. His laughter rings in the air when he talks to his son. And now, when he sleeps, his world-weary, battle-hardened edges are softer. When he sleeps, his mask slips.

He's only down for about an hour when he jolts awake, looking panicked for a moment as he blinks around the room, trying to reorient himself. "Where's Matty? Where's everyone?"

"And what am I? No one?" I try to lighten the mood as he comes awake.

After a moment of confusion, he realizes I'm joking and relaxes. Then he grins. "Oh you're someone all right."

I'm impressed with the drugs they've given him. Less than twenty-four hours since he suffered a stroke, and he's already flirting again. It's a miracle of modern science!

Answering his original question, I say, "Mateo and your mom went home for food and naps. Drew and Chloe went to work and school. I'm sticking around until they release you, so I can drive you home."

"You drew the short straw, huh?"

I laugh, and it feels nice, comfortable. But his expression sinks when he says, "Dee, I'm sorry I guilted you into staying last night. It wasn't fair of me to pressure you like that."

I appreciate the apology, but it's not necessary. "You didn't pressure me. I was pretty much on board to stay if you wanted me to. Which you did."

Rico seems surprised, which makes me sad. Despite everything, all our storied history, he can always count on me, no matter what. Have I not made that clear?

"A few weeks ago, when I woke up in the hospital and found you there, I know I gave you hell for that, but it was a comfort I needed. When I was hurting, you made sure I wasn't alone. That meant a lot to me."

Rico's grin pulls at my heart. I can feel the tug, deep down in the center of my chest. It makes me nervous. And my nervousness makes me feel defensive, so I casually tack on, "I'm just returning the favor."

"Well… Thank you." He glances down at himself. "Honestly, this is a little embarrassing though."

"What's embarrassing?"

"Being in the hospital, laid up in this bed. I feel…weak. And I don't want to be weak in front of you. When I came back to town, I wanted you to see me as a man who's *worthy* of a woman like you, and instead you get to feast your eyes on this." He fists his hospital gown for emphasis. "A weak, broken man tangled in wires and bruised all over, lying on his back in front of the woman he's actively trying to woo."

"You're trying to woo me?"

"Yeah," he frowns, "clearly I'm doing a really shitty job of it."

I come to my feet and cross to his bed, sitting on the edge. Holding his gaze so I can be sure he's listening, I tell him, "When I look at you, I don't see anything weak or broken. I see a survivor. I see a man who's experienced the worst this world has to offer, and still he has the strength to make his little boy feel safe and happy and loved."

Rico's breath huffs out of him like I've stolen it, and his expression falls. The casual humor of his smile is gone, replaced with a look that's equal parts invigoration and devastation. Clearly, I've touched a nerve.

With hands that hold more strength in them than he could manage last night, Rico laces our fingers together, staring deep into my eyes. "Dee Marie Fletcher, every single moment I get to spend with you makes me fall more in love with you than I've ever been before."

Now I'm the one made breathless. Like I'm drowning, I sink to some new depth within myself where my feelings are as murky as the bottom of the ocean. I don't know what to say.

This is the second time he's said words to this effect in the last twenty-four hours, but last night he'd thought he was dying. During his stroke, he'd declared his everlasting love for me and Matty like they would be his last words. This, though, is different. There is no duress here, only honesty between us on this hospital bed.

Now it's my turn to tell him my truth, but what is that truth? My truth is, well, complicated. I know that I love Rico, I always have, but he left me once before, and it nearly broke me. Can I trust him not to do it again? That thought sends me into a panic. But part of me wants to take that chance on him.

For too long, I've insulated myself, *isolated* myself, so no one could ever hurt me again. My mom left me for pills, and the pain of that tried to break me, but Rico was there to keep me from completely closing myself off. When I lost him, too, I buried myself in work, running into fire like a defense mechanism, keeping everyone at a distance, too far away to ever hurt me.

And it's been lonely.

Maybe now is the time to lower my defenses and try to trust again. I open my mouth like I'm going to say all of that when one of the nurses comes in to check on him and inspect the numbers on the machines. Like we've been caught, young lovers groping in secret, I pull away from Rico's grip and stand from his bed, pacing around the small room as I stretch the aches and pains out of my back.

Rico tries not to seem too disappointed by the timing of her interruption as he asks, "What's my prognosis, Patty?"

"Everything looks good. We will want to do another CT to confirm, but you seem to be responding well to the treatment. I think the doctor will be ready to release you in the morning."

"In the morning?" He fails to mask his disappointment this time.

Patty nods and gives him an emphatic smile.

"And after that?"

She blinks.

He clarifies, "When will we know *why* this happened to me?"

"Oh. Your doctor will refer you to a cardiologist and a neurologist to follow up, and they will likely order a lot of tests." She keeps talking while she works. "I'd expect they'll want to perform an ultrasound of your arteries to see if they spot any plaque that might have broken loose into your bloodstream. They will likely also order an echocardiogram of your heart, probably with a bubble study, to determine if there are any abnormalities. I'm sure they'll get to the bottom of it. In the meantime, you rest up. Your brain is doing a lot of healing right now. It needs the sleep." Patty gives Rico's shoulder a squeeze, assuring him she'll be in again when it's time.

After she's gone, we share a silent moment before Rico says, "You don't have to stay."

"What do you mean?"

"I have to spend another night here, but you don't."

"Are you kicking me out?"

"No, I just—"

"Then I'm staying." I settle back into my chair, trying to look comfortable. He smirks at me, like he's going to argue, but I jump in first. "Remember when I got chicken pox?"

Rico's face softens into a wide smile. "How could I forget? You infected me."

"You infected yourself, dummy. Always sneaking over with thermoses of chicken noodle soup."

He shrugs bashfully, and it's adorable. "You were sick, and your dad was useless. Someone needed to make sure you ate and got healthy again."

His words, those memories: they split a fissure in my chest, right through my heart. I change the subject back to him. "But then you got sick, too, so much sicker than me."

"The price of love."

Jesus, he's going to do me in. It hurts to remember how close we used to be, how I always wanted us to be, and, if I'm being honest with myself, how I want us to be again. I change the subject *again*. No more talk of love in the time of chicken pox. "I think your mom knew I was sneaking into your room at night with soup."

He smiles wide. "She did. She'd ask about you in the mornings."

I laugh. That little lady has always been too aware. We couldn't slip anything past her.

"But since you'd already had the pox, there wasn't any harm in exposing me to your healing powers."

I guffaw. It's a very awkward explosion of laughter at the thought of me with any sort of power to heal.

"I'm serious, Dee. You save people all the time. You're a healer and a hero. You always have been."

I squirm in this stupid chair, feeling incredibly uncomfortable, like I'm too large and too small for it, all at the same time. Seeming to sense my discomfort, it's Rico who changes the subject this time. "What's a bubble study?"

Oh excellent, a new subject, and one I love. "It's this really cool procedure where they blow bubbles into one chamber of your heart and watch on the echocardiograph to see if the bubbles travel to another chamber. If they see the bubbles in both atria, then that means you have a hole between the two chambers, a defect. If they don't see the bubbles come through, then they investigate other, less common, causes of your stroke. I've watched footage of a few bubble studies online. The procedure's really cool. A total miracle of modern science."

"They blow bubbles into my heart?" He looks alarmed. "Won't that kill me? I thought a bubble in the bloodstream was a bad thing. Isn't that why you guys flick the bubbles to the top when you're giving an injection—so you can push the bubbles out with the plunger?"

That's a lot of questions. Where to start… "Okay, first, that whole thing about flicking the needle is actually to ensure we're getting an accurate dosage of whatever we're injecting. And the bubbles we're talking about in a bubble study are tiny. You know, 'Tiny Bubbles' like that Don Ho song."

I expect more of a laugh from him, but his train of thought must have derailed somewhere along the way. Rico clenches his fists around the edge of his blanket. It's an old tell; often the only way I could ever read Rico's emotions was by the position of his hands. Right now, he's freaking out.

I return to sit on his bed, clasping my hands over his, and he lets me lace our fingers together as I try again to comfort him. "Rico, seriously, they are tiny. They're like a lather, super itty-bitty. And they do no harm—I promise. They just help the physician see if there's a hole in your heart." Like I'm the chicken noodle soup fairy again, I say. "If you want, I can come with you to your appointment. So you're not alone."

He stares at me a moment, then smiles. "Will you hold my hand through it?"

I try not to smile back, but I can't help it. "Yeah, okay."

CHAPTER 18
RICO

Her text reads: **When are they going to blow bubbles into your heart?**

Another text immediately follows: **This is Dee, by the way.**

It's cute that she thinks I don't have her number programmed into my phone. Or that I've talked to anyone else about the goddamn bubbles in my heart. I shiver at the reminder. To distract myself, I fuck with her: **Dee? Dee who?**

Her reply comes immediately: **Dee Snyder, from Twisted Sister, of course. Here to rock you like a hurricane.**

Oh, sweet, naïve Dee, so clueless about music history: **That wasn't Twisted Sister. That was the Scorpions. Twisted Sister were the ones who were not gonna take it.**

How do you know so much about '80s hair metal?

Older brothers.

Totally awesome, dude!

I love texting with her like this. It reminds me of when we were young, texting back and forth after lights out because mamá set a no-more-talking-on-the-phone-after-ten curfew on us but never thought to set a texting curfew too.

I throw a metal hand emoji her way, knowing it will bother her. And right on cue, my phone chimes as her response comes in: **Oh no! Demerits for using an emoji, Rico Suave.**

Ugh. She's dusted off that awful old nickname from my junior-high days. In revenge, I fill my next text with a whole string of adult-themed emojis. Everything from the tongue and water droplets to the eggplant and peach. Covering all the bases in harmless-yet-lewd little icons.

What are you, twelve? Bye boi.

I'm not sure where else to go with this except, well, answering her initial question: **They're blowing bubbles into my heart tomorrow. 3:30.**

Great. I'll pick you up at 3.

It takes all my restraint not to text back, "It's a date." This is not a date, jackass. It's a scary medical procedure whereby they blow motherfucking bubbles into my motherfucking heart. I shiver at the thought.

I know that Dee is only coming along as a favor to me, but I'm so relieved she'll be there. I'm too old—and manly—to drag my sixty-eight-year-old mother to these sorts of things, but I didn't want to go alone. Knowing Dee will be with me sets my mind at ease. I smile, almost looking forward to it now, and text her: **See you then.**

⎯⋀⋀⎯♡⎯⋀⋀⎯

"How did you get the shrapnel in your shoulder?"

I blink at Dee's random question and glance around the waiting room of my cardiologist's office, a little lost.

She elaborates, "Was it the same attack that killed John and injured Theresa?"

I'm impressed she remembers John's name. Though, it makes sense that she would: his death had a profound effect on me, and her as well, considering it's why I broke us up… On second thought, I'm not at all surprised she remembers his name. And of course she remembers Theresa's name. It carries baggage too.

With a sigh, I explain, "Yeah, same attack. I was far enough from the blast to survive but close enough to take some damage to my right shoulder. The doctors removed what they could without causing further damage, but a few pieces remain."

I rub my shoulder, where I can still feel the faint scars from that night in Kandahar. The memories of the worst night of my life are sewn up in those scars.

"So you weren't discharged with your injury?"

"No. I was treated at a field hospital and returned to duty within a week. I wasn't discharged until Theresa's neglect landed Matty in foster care."

She stares at me for a moment, as if she's considering what to think about that. "But you have full custody now?"

I smile and nod, so relieved to finally be free from that nightmare with full custody and a divorce. "Yes. Thank God."

She smiles sweetly and says, "Mateo is lucky to have you for a dad."

That's probably the kindest compliment anyone has ever given me, and it's not true at all. I have no clue what I'm doing or how to be a good father. I moved back home so mamá could help keep me from drowning under the pressure of failing Matty…again.

But then I remember Dee's dad, and I don't feel like such a failure. Her mom had been addicted to pills, too, so much so that she over-dosed when we were kids. When she died, I felt like some kind of subject-matter expert because I'd already lost my dad. But Dee's loss was so different from mine. Hers was a different kind of tragedy with a different kind of grief.

And her surviving parent was nothing like my mom. Mark was a mess. From what I've seen since I returned to town, Mark is *still* a mess. Dee has always been the adult in that relationship. I imagine she'll understand more than most people when I say, "I regret the second chance I gave Theresa. I was naïve about what addiction can do to a person and how much she could hurt Matty with her empty promises and neglect."

Dee clasps my hand in hers. "You were trying to do the right thing. Sometimes, it's hard to recognize when doing the right thing is actually the wrong choice."

I raise a brow, knowing the answer before I ask, "You speak from experience?"

She bites her lip and plucks at the little freckle on her chin, finally saying, "I've tried more times than I can count to help my dad get sober. After so many broken promises, I had to pull away. For my own sanity, I can't keep believing him when he lies. Now, I just let him live the life he wants, even if it means witnessing him slowly drink himself to death."

I hate this reminder that all of Dee's important relationships have ended in disappointment and abandonment, including her relationship with me. But I'm back, and maybe that counts for something. I squeeze her hand in mine. It's my left hand, which is still somewhat numb from the stroke, so I have to squeeze extra hard. It makes her smile, like she recognizes the added effort.

The door to the doctor's office swings open, and a woman hollers my name. Dee stands, and with our hands still linked, she helps me stand too. I'm a little less steady on my feet these days, but not too bad. Technically, I don't need to hold her hand as we walk to the exam room, but now that I have her in my grasp, I don't ever want to let her go.

The room we end up in is small and dark, with a narrow bed in the corner and a large monitor and console beside it. I take off my T-shirt, then sit down on the bed so a nurse can get an IV into my arm.

"Bet you're tired of us blood suckers, aren't ya?" she jokes.

She's not wrong. My laugh comes out sounding strange. The echocardiograph technician easily senses my nervousness and kindly explains the steps of today's procedure. First, she'll do a normal echocardiogram. Then, the nurse will administer a saline push for the bubble study.

I only half understand because I'm only half listening. Mostly, I stare at Dee, who watches me from the corner, like a fly on the wall, trying to stay out of the way. Her presence is more of a comfort to me than anything.

So I keep my eyes on her as we start the procedure. After I lie down on that little bed, the technician rubs some lube on my chest and starts moving the wand against my skin. The rhythm of my heartbeat fills the room, and Dee's grin widens. She moves her gaze from me to the monitor, and I turn my head to look too.

It's strangely *fascinating*.

That's my heart, there on the monitor in black and white, pumping my lifeblood through me. I'm staring inside myself at so much movement. I'm hearing inside myself, and it's very noisy.

I think back to those lonely, quiet nights in the vast silent wilds of Afghanistan, staring up at the stars, as the world lay still all around me. But it was an illusion. Nothing was still then. The Earth moved through the cosmos, turning on its axis, as creatures tunneled and sifted through the dirt all around me; everything was always moving. And inside me now, blood pumps through my veins, electricity snaps along my neurons, and nothing is still. Nothing is ever still.

"Okay, let's start the bubble study," the technician says. "You'll see the bubble solution enter this chamber here. If there is a hole, then a small trail of bubbles will enter this chamber over here." She points to the sections of my beating heart on the monitor as she explains what's about to happen.

I follow the technician's every word as the nurse stands behind me, working a pair of plungers to push saline from one tube to the other until it's a bubbly froth. At the same time, the technician makes sure the probe is positioned well against my chest, then starts a recording on the monitor as she instructs the nurse to push the froth into my IV.

The nurse pushes a plunger on one of the tubes, and on the monitor, I see the moment the saline fizz reaches my heart. Bubbles fill the first chamber, as expected. The thin stream that escapes into the next chamber is a surprise.

"Holy shit, there's a hole," I say, stunned.

I glance over to Dee, who is just as stunned as I am, eyes wide, jaw hanging open. In that instant, we've found it: the reason I've lived for nearly thirty years and survived a damn war, only to come home and have a stroke during sex. I have a motherfucking hole in my motherfucking heart!

The nurse and technician have me perform a few more tasks, like coughing and holding my breath, while they do additional tests, but I've seen what I need to see. I know the cause of all my troubles.

My heart is broken.

"Okay. Question," Rico starts as the doctor finishes explaining his heart condition and outlining next steps. He squeezes my hand, which he's been holding since they finished the echocardiogram. Once they'd removed his IV, Rico sat up, wiped the lube off his chest so he could slip his shirt back on, and took my hand. He hasn't let me go since. And I haven't minded. Clearing his throat, he asks his question: "Can we have sex again?"

I choke, cough. *Subtle, Dee. Not awkward at all.*

But what *the fuck*, Rico? Your heart doctor does not need to know our business. Then again, when you consider it was our *business* that caused his stroke, it's a valid question.

Rico's cardiologist, Dr. Thomas, looks between us and answers professionally. "Yes. You're on so many blood thinners, you won't have another clot like the one that caused the stroke. I encourage exercise. It's good for your heart."

"You heard the man—it's good for my heart." Rico winks at me when we get outside, walking toward my car at the back of the lot.

"Seriously, Rico?" I can finally laugh out loud, which I do, freely. "In your dreams, Stroke Boy."

"Stroke Boy, I like that." He bites his bottom lip as he starts gyrating his hips and pantomiming like he's fucking an invisible woman from behind. "You like that, baby? You like what Stroke Boy's got for you?"

"Stop it! You're embarrassing yourself." I pop the locks on the car and go to the passenger side to make sure Rico doesn't need any help getting in. Despite his big talk, Rico moves a little slower than before the stroke, a little less steady on his feet. Leaning on the door frame, I add, "I don't do gentle, Rico. With all those blood thinners you're on, if I fuck you, you'll be bruised for days."

"God, that's hot. Say more." Rico winks at me again.

I slam his door shut and move around, sliding into the driver's seat as I say, "Bruise, contusion, welt, swelling—"

"Mmm, swelling—"

"Lesion, lump—"

"You heard the doctor. He *encourages* exercise."

I roll my eyes at him as I start the car and drive us back to Inez's house. Rico laughs, and it's such a great sound. I like this side of him. Since the stroke, it's like he's shed some of the burden he'd carried for so long. Maybe it's a side effect of a major medical crisis, but he seems to be prioritizing the important things in his life, and obviously sex is high on the list.

"It's church night." He's still negotiating. "The house will be empty. I could make you dinner."

"You're still recovering from the last time you made me dinner. "

"I never even got to feed you then. I owe you a meal."

It's tempting. Very tempting.

I turn onto Lazy River Road and check out all the activity over at

Drew and Chloe's construction site. Looks like they're installing windows today. I slow to turn into Inez's drive and stop, staring at the driveway in bewilderment.

It's packed. Instead of just Inez and Rico's cars resting in front of the house, there are four vehicles cluttering up the space. There's barely enough room for me to tuck my Charger in and keep her ass out of the road.

"What's going on?" I look over to Rico, who's smiling wide.

"My brothers," he says, and as soon as I've stopped the car, he fumbles with the door latch to get out. At the top of the drive, his two big brothers come bursting out the front door and jog over for a reunion.

I stay back, locking up the car as a Rodriguez family reunion happens a few feet away. Rico is much younger than his brothers—his mom calling him a sorpresa placentera, or pleasant surprise—so they've always babied him. They would take him everywhere they went, like he was their mascot. And when I came along, so was I.

I haven't seen Manny Junior or Javi in years. They're such men now, with gray at their temples and laugh lines bracketing their smiles.

"What the hell are you assholes doing here?" Rico asks Javi as they hug.

"¡Ay Dios mio! Such foul language, hermanito. Don't let mamá hear you say that," Manny chimes in.

Javi says, "Of course we're here. When our baby brother goes down with a stroke, he can expect a visit."

Rico smirks, seeming a little sad from the reminder of his current condition but still happy to be standing arm in arm with his big brothers.

Manny looks my way, and his brows hit his hairline. "Do my eyes deceive me?" He comes at me with his hands out like he wants to pinch my cheeks. "Javi, would you look at this? It's little Dee Dee Fletcher all grown up!"

I shake my head, sure I'm blushing bright red as the Rodriguez brothers turn their attention on me, swooping me into meaty bear hugs.

"Good to see you, girl," one of them says. "You keeping our little brother in line?"

"That's an impossible task, and you know it."

They laugh, and with a snicker, Javi adds, "Well if anyone can do it, it'd be you, chica mona."

I pull away from the hugs, ready to let the family enjoy their reunion in peace, when Inez steps out of the house looking vibrant in an aqua pantsuit. She holds Mateo's hand in hers, and to everyone's surprise, that little devil runs right past his dad and his uncles to tackle me around the legs in a hug.

"Dee, my tios are here," he says to me with a gigantic grin.

"I see that."

"And abuela let me help make the enchiladas."

"Well that sounds yummy."

"You can have one, if you want."

This little boy is too sweet for this world. "Well, I think tonight is a family night. So you'll get to have two enchiladas!"

I look up at Rico and his family, a little surprised by how they're all staring at me like I've said something shocking or profound.

It's Inez who says, "Dee, stay for dinner. It will be like old times." All of Inez's boys nod, both generations of them.

"Oh, I couldn't intrude, this is family—"

"And you're family," Inez insists. "Now come inside before we feed the next generation of mosquitoes."

Everyone else laughs at her joke, but I'm struck dumb by one particular part of her statement. I'm *family?*

Inez doesn't wait for me to accept the invite; she just turns and leads us into the house like ducklings in a row. Mateo wraps his hand around a few of my fingers and pulls me inside too.

Once we've taken seats around the table, said our grace, and filled our plates, the conversation turns serious. Above the ambient clatter of cutlery against ceramic, Javi asks Rico, "How are you, hermanito?"

Rico finishes cutting Mateo's enchiladas into bite-size pieces before answering. "Better every day. I've been going to speech therapy for my aphasia."

"What's aphasia?" one of the brothers asks.

"It's where you have trouble expressing or understanding language. Like, the other day, I was trying to say the word 'eleven' but the word 'yellow' came out instead."

"Weird."

"Yeah."

"As for the physical symptoms, I have most of the sensation back on my left side, except my left foot still has some numbness, and it feels like I have a string wrapped around my pinky toe."

"Weird," they say again.

I have to bite my lips together to keep from laughing at their one-word responses. Despite Javi's job as a television script writer, the Rodriguez brothers have never been particularly verbose.

"Yeah," Rico agrees, in an equally succinct reply.

"How's work? Are they letting you take time off?" Javi finally puts his wordsmithing skills to use.

"Right now I work half days and mostly from home. My editor has me working on an in-depth article about the stroke. So I've been doing a lot of research into all this."

"That's great. Do they know what caused it? Is it like Dad's stroke?" Manuel asks between bites of food.

"I've requested Dad's medical records to see exactly what caused his. As for me: it turns out my heart is broken."

The whole family gasps, especially Mateo, whose eyes are like saucers as he looks up at his dad in absolute terror.

Rico, really? Did you have to be so dramatic about it?

"His condition is actually extremely common," I pipe up.

Everyone turns to me, hoping my news will be less scary than Rico's cryptic announcement. So I dive deep into an explanation of what Rico and I learned today at his appointment. This stuff is interesting to me, but not to everyone else, so I try to keep a lightweight academic tone as I pretty much repeat verbatim what the doctor told us.

"He either has a PFO or an ASD. Both are very common and easily fixable. PFO stands for patent foramen ovale. It's a hole with a flap over it that everyone has when we're born. It's between the upper chambers of the heart, and it's how blood circulates through the body without the use of lungs when we're in utero. Once we're born, and we take that first breath"—I take a big breath to demonstrate—"that flap slams shut, and over time, it grows closed. Except, in about twenty-five percent of the population, it doesn't close properly."

"A quarter of the population?" Javi asks.

I nod.

"Wow."

"It doesn't always result in a stroke. Some people live their entire lives and never know they have a PFO. But if one is detected, like in the case of a stroke, it's easy to correct.

"On the other hand, ASD, which stands for atrial septal defect, is an actual birth defect. It means the chambers of the heart didn't fully grow closed before birth. The treatment for it is similar to a PFO. So now Rico has to go back to the doctor next week for an esophageal echocardiogram. This will help the doctor determine which type Rico has. Once that's known, all that's left is to close the hole."

I stop talking and take a large bite of my enchilada. I glance around the table, where everyone is staring at me, sort of blinking. Hmm, did I lose them somewhere along the way? Maybe I was too technical in my descriptions.

Before I can try again, Rico bellows, "As I was saying, my heart is broken."

I smirk at him and swallow my food. "And it's easily mendable."

CHAPTER 20
RICO

She's humming that song again.

"Tell me about it," I say as we walk off the enchiladas and tres leches, strolling up Lazy River Road toward the old oak tree.

"What?"

"That song. You've been humming it all day."

"What song?"

"I Hate Myself for Loving You."

She blinks at me, then her eyes go wide, realizing I'm right.

I know she's a Joan Jett fan, but I have to wonder if her earworm choice has a deeper meaning. "Want to talk about it?"

"Talk about what?"

"How you feel about us. How you feel about me. The weather. Whatever you need to talk about, I'll listen."

She doesn't say anything for a long time. We walk slowly up the hill under a blanket of stars. It's probably too warm tonight for a leisurely stroll, but I'm enjoying this time alone with Dee nonetheless.

Her voice cuts through the night when she says, "I've always feared earthquakes."

That's random. Does an earthquake qualify as weather?

"The thought of having the earth shift beneath my feet seems terrifying. Life is full of shifting things. The earth should be solid, dependable, never move.

"That's what your letter felt like to me. You were my rock, my constant. And then you were…gone. I tried to write to you after that, and you never wrote back. You vanished from my life, as if you had died. Except you didn't die. You left intentionally, and that hurt worse."

Fuck. "I'm so sorry."

"I know," she says wistfully.

"No, I don't think you do know. I don't think I've really told you." I stop walking. Our tree is off to the left, a few paces through the field. It feels like as good a place as any for this to be said, so I take her hands in mine. "I love you, Dee. I've always loved you. But I was an idiot. I thought I needed to *live a little* before I settled into a small-town life. It wasn't until that night, when I wrote the letter, that I realized how stupid I'd been. That I already had everything I was searching for, and I'd left it when I left *you.*

"But by then, it was too late. I was sure I couldn't come back to this, certain I wouldn't come back at all. It broke my heart to imagine I'd never get to see you again." I raise my hand to stroke her cheek, needing that connection. "I thought I'd never be able to touch you again or feel your breath on my neck or taste your orgasms… All of it was over for me.

"I was miserable about it, so I started drinking—which was strictly forbidden for service members in Afghanistan, but we found a way, of course we found a way—and I fucked up a lot in those days, but especially when I fucked Theresa. That was the night when I broke my own heart. It felt like such a betrayal to you. Even though I'd already sent you that stupid letter, it wasn't until that night that I knew there was no going back to the life I'd had before.

"But that night gave me a new life as Matty's father. And suddenly, I had this incredibly important reason to survive, to stop fucking up. My whole existence became about him. He was the reason I fought. He was the reason I survived. And he was the reason I came home."

I see the hurt in her eyes, like she's wondering why *she* wasn't reason enough to fight, survive, and come home. I try to explain better, but it's hard to put this part into words. "You're so strong. I knew you'd be okay without me. With Matty, it's different. Fatherhood is a different kind of love. There's a heavy weight to it, a terrifying responsibility that I've never known before. It is all consuming. My love for Matty replaced everything else, for years. And I have no regrets about that."

She smiles, and it's genuine, like she understands, even when I don't completely understand it myself.

"But then, I moved back here, and on my first day at a new job, I got the call all parents dread—finding out my son was hurt. And when I walked into his hospital room, you were there.

"Seeing you that day—that was *my* earthquake. It shook me to my core because in an instant, I knew I'd never stopped loving you, and I never will. And every moment I've spent with you since then just strengthens my resolve."

I wrap my arms around her waist and bring her closer, staring deep into her beautiful green eyes. "Dee, I loved the girl you were, so much. But this woman you've become—she's amazing. *You're* amazing. And I'm desperate to earn back your love and trust."

Dee furrows her brow and purses her lips and, in a whisper nearly snatched away by the breeze, says, "I'm not as strong as you think. I fell apart without you."

Fuck. Her words gut me. I press my forehead against hers and just start groveling. "I'm sorry. I'm beyond sorry. That word is too small to even begin to cover how sorry I am. Hurting you—I regret it...so much. I regret that I didn't understand how special we were together. If I could change one thing in this life, it would be how I hurt you, how I ruined *us*."

Dee sniffs and wipes her eyes.

I pull away, just enough to help wipe away some of the wetness from her cheeks. And the sight of her like this—crying in my arms, crying *because* of what I did—brings tears to my own eyes. I sniff and wipe them away before I finally ask the question I desperately need her to answer. "Do you think you can ever forgive me? I'll understand if you can't, but I hope—"

"I already did." She blinks up at me, and the stars shine in her eyes.

I'm stunned, speechless.

Without another word, Dee turns away, wiping away the last of her tears as she stares across the dark field at our tree. And then she walks out toward it, traipsing into the brush and bramble to stand beneath the shelter of its wide branches.

I follow her into the wild scrub brush. It's a little slow going for me as I'm extra careful where I put my feet. Despite some residual weakness on the left side, I haven't fallen since the stroke. I don't plan to start now.

"When did you forgive me?" I ask as I watch her trace the indentations I made years ago when I carved our initials into this old giant.

"In the hospital, after your stroke, I realized I don't hate you. I never did. And there is a part of me that understands why you left."

"You do?" *Please tell me. I'd like to know.*

"You were right. Our lives were small back then. And these days, it's unusual to stay solid and true with the person you fell in love with in the third grade. Our lives aren't small anymore, Rico. Even though I stayed in Krause, I've traveled. I've lived. You survived a war, and then you survived a stroke. Sitting in your hospital room got me thinking about how when someone matters to you and they fuck up, you have to decide if their fuckup is forgivable or not, and if it is forgivable, then fucking forgive them because life is too short to stay mad about the past. So anyways… I forgive you."

She turns away from the tree to face me, and her eyes appear almost translucent in the darkness, like she's completely open, letting me see all the way into her heart and soul. And what I see there is warmth and sweetness.

I move toward her, wanting to wrap her in my arms, to grab hold of her and never let go.

"Do you forgive yourself?" she asks, and the question hits me like a jolt to the heart.

My God, *do* I forgive myself? *No.* Out loud, I admit, "I'm still working on it."

It's probably not the most satisfying answer, but it's the truth. And, with that said, I kiss her.

This kiss is different from the others we've shared since my return home. This kiss is like a language, with meaning, not like our devouring sex-starved kisses. There is more than feeling in this kiss; there's emotion.

But there's a lot of feeling, too, and I'm so fucking hard for her right now it hurts. Still connected with a kiss, I try to lower us to the ground.

Dee pulls away to ask, "What are you doing?"

"I want to make love to you."

"Here?" She frowns. "On the ground?"

I try to make it sound romantic. "On the spot where we shed our virginity."

She's not buying it. "Rico, there are snakes out here, and scorpions, and tarantulas. I'm not seventeen anymore. I need you to *make love* to me indoors, in a proper bed."

"Matty is sleeping in my *proper* bed while my brothers are in town."

"Bummer," she says in a teasing tone, trying and failing to hide her grin.

I like that things are light between us again, so easy. Even after that heavy conversation, she's clearly feeling playful.

I play, too, wrapping my arms around her waist and swaying to a silent song as I commiserate. "Tell me about it. My brothers have always cramped my style, but this is extreme, even for them. Do you have any idea how desperate I am to hear you orgasm right now? It's one of my top five favorite sounds."

"What are the other four?"

I show her a hand to count them on my fingers: "Matty's laughter, your laughter, mamá's laughter, the coyotes, and your orgasms."

"You rank my orgasms beneath the coyotes?"

"That wasn't a ranked list."

She gives me a devious grin. "Nice try, Stroke Boy, but I heard what I heard."

Right on cue, one of the neighborhood coyotes howls into the night. We listen as another responds.

"Hmm, it is a nice sound. I can see why you ranked it above my orgasms."

I lean into her, pressing her back against our tree and brushing her hair over her shoulder so I can whisper into her ear. "I don't know. I think I need to hear you come again, for comparison's sake."

"For science." She giggles.

"Yes. Please let me finger you for science."

Now she laughs. "Such a romantic."

"You want romance? I can do that too." I move in, ready for action, reciting a few lines from Shakespeare as I cup my palm against her pussy, grinding the heel of my hand to make her whimper.

I love the way she turns soft in my arms, her eyelids sinking to half-mast as a moan passes her lips. "That's it, baby. Let me have this."

She nods, and I slip my hand inside her jeans, maneuvering in the tight space to find her warm and wet and waiting for me. *Fuck.*

Normally, I'd use my left hand for works of dexterity, but I don't want the numbness on my left side to ruin this for her or me. So it's my right tonight, baby. Lucky for us, I'm ambidextrous.

Dee welcomes my advance, shifting her legs to give me space to work. I slide my middle finger inside, and her breath catches. She whimpers, and that sound sends me over the edge. I'm hard as fucking stone as she mewls and writhes and drips down my finger. Her weight hangs from where she's wrapped her arms around my neck, and her lips seek mine as she angles for a kiss.

When I slip a second finger inside, she goes boneless, and her breath turns ragged as she clings to me, her fingers tangled in my hair. She pulls away from the kiss to watch me and let me watch her. I've always *loved* to watch this part: her eyes go wide, and her mouth falls open as she gasps and cries out in ecstasy. It's music to my ears.

Taking my fingers out of her jeans, I slip them into my mouth and lick them clean as I say, "I definitely rank the sound of your orgasm over coyotes."

Dee watches me savor her flavor and gives me a look. It's *that* look, the one that tells me she's turned on again, ready for more.

"Come on," she says and clasps my free hand in hers as she starts tugging me back toward the road.

"Where are we going?"

"My back seat."

I laugh. "What happened to 'indoors, in a proper bed'?"

"We work with what we've got."

She unlocks her way into the purple Charger parked farthest from the house, affording us at least a little privacy. As soon as she's inside, she slips her shirt off and tosses it into the front. I slide in behind her, closing the car door as quietly as I can, then my shirt joins hers as I start to strip. Beside me, Dee is trying to yank her shoes and jeans off at the same time. At least she's finally out of her boot, but still, it's a mess. I help, tugging her sneakers off as she kicks and wiggles her way out of the rest. All that's left is her bra, and when she reaches to pop it off, too, I grab her wrists and hold them there, behind her back.

"I'll take care of this one." I slide across the seat, squeezing my grip on her arms, demonstrating my control. She doesn't seem to mind as I run the tip of my nose up the column of her neck, breathing her in. She shivers when I run my tongue back down, then use my teeth to grab hold of the strap of her bra and pull it off her shoulder.

Still in my grasp, she squirms and sighs and gets one leg over my lap, straddling me in the middle of the back seat. I run my tongue down her chest to the edge of her bra, a pale silk that's almost as soft as her skin. With my teeth again, I tug the cup down to reveal her tight nipple, rising and falling with her heavy breath.

I take it into my mouth, laving it with my tongue, sucking and nibbling on that tight, pink tip. Her breath goes ragged, and she moans so sweetly, I do it all again and again until I turn my attention to the other strap of her bra, tugging it down her arm so she's completely exposed to me.

And then, I stare. "You're so beautiful, baby. You take my breath away," I finally say, trying to sound sweet before the beast in me takes over. Which he does, with a growl from the back of my throat as I suck her nipple into my mouth.

When I release my grip on her wrists to pop the snap on her bra, Dee uses the opportunity to reach for the button and zipper of my jeans. I pull her bra the rest of the way off and run my hands all over her gorgeous body, caressing her until I reach her ass and squeeze.

"You have a magnificent ass."

"I run a lot of stairs," she responds as she pulls my cock out of the confines of my jeans. "Oh, baby, is this all for me?"

She's so sexy when she talks dirty, her hand stroking me from stem to tip.

"Every inch of me is yours," I say as I slide my hands down her ass until my fingers reach between her thighs to touch and tease her pussy. "You're so wet for me."

She makes a sound like a purr, which revs me hotter, but her hands freeze midstroke, and she frowns at me. "Do you have a condom?"

I freeze too. "Not on me. Do you?"

She pulls away to shake her head. We stare at each other for a long moment, considering options. I have a box of condoms in a drawer in my room, but I'd have to sneak past my family and into the room where my son sleeps to get them.

After a moment, during which she's still stroking my cock, Dee says, "I'm on birth control, and I was tested for STIs after leaving my last boyfriend."

"I haven't had sex with anyone except you in five years."

She blinks at me. "Really?"

I nod, but otherwise I don't move. Watching her, I wait for her to decide what happens next.

Slowly, she strokes my cock again and shifts her hips closer to me, then slides down my length. She gasps as she takes me all the way in and starts to move.

"Oh, fuck, yes, baby, you feel so good, so goddamn perfect," I groan.

Dee wraps her arms around my neck, and she stares deep into my eyes, connecting us there too. Our gazes are steady, locked together as we start to move harder, faster. I grab her ass again and squeeze as I push deeper inside her. She rides me rougher, too, her hot breath warming my cheek as she takes everything I give her.

She moves her arms from my neck and presses her palms to the roof of her car, balancing above me as she fucks us both senseless. Good Lord, this view is heaven. She's a goddess, Aphrodite fucking me so good in the back seat of her car.

Her pussy tightens, and she throws her head back to cry out as she comes. The feel of her, the sight of her, the sounds she makes; it all has me coming, too, instant and all-consuming.

I see stars, and for a moment I panic. After all, my last orgasm sent a clot crashing through my brain. This orgasm is even better. This one could kill me. But as I come down from ecstasy, I know I'm okay. I'm more than okay. I'm fan-fucking-tastic.

With a sexy, breathy sigh, she collapses against me, and I wrap my arms around her, savoring the feel of her as I kiss her forehead and stroke her hair behind her ear. When we've caught our breath, she pulls away enough to say, "Hi."

I grin, because I completely understand. "Hi."

She smiles, and it's like the start of something new between us. We have so much history, all that baggage, but this moment between us— it's different than every moment we've shared before. It's calm and peaceful and nice in some strange sort of way. I like it. No, I love it.

Stroking my fingers across her cheek, I tell her, "I love you, more than I've ever loved you before."

Her eyes dance over my face, like she's looking for something to say, but she doesn't find it, and that's okay. She doesn't have to say anything. Right now, more than anything, I need her to hear me and trust me, so I look deep into her eyes when I say, "I won't fuck it up this time. I promise you. You possess my heart. You always have. You always will. Whatever you want or need from me, it's yours."

Her eyes sparkle in the dark with unshed tears. She presses her palms to my cheeks, and softly, sweetly, she kisses me.

When I slip back into the house, I expect everyone to be asleep. I'd said I was going to walk Dee out while my brothers tucked Matty in and read to him. Mamá is usually early to rise and early to bed too. So it surprises me when I find her in the kitchen, sitting at the table with a crossword from the paper in front of her.

"Did you have a nice time walking Dee to her car?"

Busted. "I did."

I sit in the seat across from her as she says, "I'm happy."

There's no context to what she means, but I think I know. She has her whole family here, under her roof. Even if the reason for this reunion isn't altogether good, it's still good to be all together.

But when she explains, she surprises me. "I'm happy because I think you're happy. You haven't been happy in such a long time, but since you came back home, you're a new man."

I agree. "I think, for the first time in my life, I have my priorities straight."

"Good." She nods resolutely. "When are you going to marry her?"

"I… Uh… Wow, mamá… What?"

"You need her, mijo. Mateo needs her."

I'm not inclined to disagree, but I'm too exhausted to keep this conversation going. I stand and kiss her cheek. "Right now, what I need is sleep. Buenas noches, mamá."

I strip off my shirt as I walk down the hall, needing a shower to wash the long day and hot sex off me. As quietly as I can, I slip into my bedroom, grabbing a fresh pair of boxers, then go to the bathroom to clean up. When I come back, I make sure to keep the door cracked and the hall light on and dump my clothes into the hamper. But when I look to my son, I see his dark eyes looking back at me.

"Hey, buddy, you still awake?"

He nods, and I slide into the bed beside him, encouraging him to cuddle with me.

With a sniff of his hair and a kiss on his forehead, I ask him, "Everything okay?"

"Daddy, is your heart broken?"

Oh, what a question; so many layers to unpack. But I know what he means, and I'm wrecked with guilt about it. Joking at dinner was an insensitive coping mechanism, and now as I look into my son's frightened eyes, I regret every word of it.

"I'm sorry I made that dumb joke at dinner. It wasn't very funny, was it?" I shake my head, and he does too. I squeeze him a little tighter and say, "Daddy's heart is just fine. You don't need to worry about me, okay, big guy?" It's not entirely true, of course, and I'm not sure what the protocol is for lying to your child in order to ease their mind, but I don't see any need to worry him over something so completely out of his control, and mine. I pound a fist on my chest like Tarzan. "See? Healthy as an ox."

"You won't go away like Mommy did?"

My guilt rachets up further. It's been difficult to talk to Matty about his Mom's incarceration. How do you explain the concept of prison to a six-year-old kid? In two years, when his mom is up for parole, he'll be old enough that we can discuss what happened, and he can decide if he'll have a relationship with her or not. Until then, I should probably find a qualified family therapist to help us navigate these fears he's feeling.

Noted.

For now, I simply say, "I won't go away. I'm here to stay. I promise. So stop your worrying, and let's get some sleep. Okay?"

"Okay."

He seems at ease, like all he needed were some comforting words he could trust. And, God, I hope he can trust my words. I hope Mateo has his dad for many decades to come. I know what it's like to grow up without a father, and Matty is already having to learn what it's like to grow up without a mother. I need to be okay, for him.

"I love you, Daddy."

I kiss the top of his head. "I love you, too, Matty. With all my heart."

It's been a long shift. What is it about the dog days of summer? Like the whole state of Texas spontaneously combusts, and we're running around putting out the fires—literally and otherwise.

"Take a small sip of water, Mr. Suarez," I instruct the eighty-two-year-old man as he sits on a bench in the scant shade of a live oak tree in front of the county courthouse. Drew applies a cold compress to the back of his neck while we wait for EMS to transport him to the hospital for treatment of heat exhaustion.

There are too many elders in this town without air-conditioning. I have half a mind to play the lotto, win, and use my winnings to buy everyone some cold air.

As an ambulance pulls to the curb, a familiar Dodge Charger slides up behind it, and out pops my favorite local reporter.

"Dee, handle the press," Watts orders, and everyone chuckles.

I roll my eyes as I walk across the crispy courthouse lawn, eyeing Rico up and down. The way he slants his head and watches me, the way he leans against the hood of his Charger: God, he's a hunk. Like an old-school hunk. Like that 1970s Cosmo centerfold of Burt Reynolds but clothed, with more muscles, and less body hair.

Then his passenger door pops open, and a woman in a summer dress and a floppy sun hat steps out. For a millisecond—one of the longest milliseconds of my adult life—my mind rockets to all the worst conclusions. Is this Mateo's mom, back to claim her family? Or is this some other woman who owns a piece of his heart? Is he here to hurt me…again?

That's when a fluffy little white cloud of a dog hops out of the car and circles the woman's feet, wagging his tail and barking excitedly. Oh, holy shit, is this who I think it is?

The woman approaches, and her little dog follows. I crouch, and the curious fella comes right over to me, letting me scoop him up into a hug.

"Leroy, look at you! So handsome without all that smoky soot in your fur."

"Thanks to you," the woman, who I now recognize as Pamela from the bathtub, says.

I twist my neck this way and that to keep Leroy from licking my mouth as I casually reply, "Just part of the job."

Technically, it was *not* part of the job. In fact, I went against direct orders when I went in search of Leroy. Watts gave me hell about it once I was out of the hospital. But the injury and the reprimand feel worth it to me now as I cuddle this wiggly little lovebug in my arms.

"Well, it's hero's work to me," Pamela says as she hugs me, squeezing her dog between us. "I'm forever grateful that you saved my baby. Thank you. Thank you. A thousand times, thank you."

The hot weather pinks my cheeks, and the blinding sun makes my eyes water. That's what it is. I'm certainly not blushing with embarrassment and on the verge of tears.

With the paramedics tending to Mr. Suarez, my crew comes over to greet Pamela and love on Leroy. If Drew is our Catman, then Rooster is the Dog Dude of our crew. The guy adores every dog he meets, and Leroy is no exception. He pulls the squirmy little pooch out of my arms to get him all hyped-up with head scratches and baby talk.

I take the opportunity to slip away from the crowd to where Rico watches everything from the shade. "I was interviewing her for a follow-up to the fire piece, and she mentioned wanting to thank you for what you did."

I nod and mimic his pose, my arms crossed over my chest, watching the action from here. He leans in, just enough that I hear him when he whispers, "Just so you know, I saw the flash of jealousy in your eyes."

I don't give him the reaction he wants. I don't give him any reaction at all. Nope. No reaction. Just watching my crew cuddle a dog.

"You thought I was with another woman, didn't you?"

I try to ignore him some more. Try and fail. With a scowl, I answer, "I can't imagine you'd be dumb enough to bring your other women around me."

With a heavy sigh, he turns to face me, blocking my view of everyone else. "There will never be another woman, Dee. You were my first, you'll be my last. You're my always."

He's said that before, a few times, but always when we were naked and tangled together in bed. For some reason, hearing him say it here feels different. Like the words take on a new shine in the sunlight, they sound louder on the hot breeze, and they mean more when said while we're fully dressed and surrounded by my crew, in the center of our town.

You're my always.

Those words echo in my head, and I love the sound of them. I love the idea of them. I want them to be true.

When Rico first turned up in town, any affection I'd shown him was left over from before. We were just tying up loose ends, exercising old demons. But somewhere along the way, it changed; *I* changed. My feelings toward Rico changed too. Now, this thing between us feels new. It's no longer a remnant of our past that we cling to when we're lonely or horny; it's a step into the future, a future he wants to share with me. And every moment I spend with Rico, it's a future I want to share with him too.

"Okay," I say dumbly because I'm not ready to say *any* of that other stuff out loud.

Rico's mouth quirks up in half a grin, like he heard all that other stuff anyway. "When are you off work?"

"Shift ends at noon." I shrug. "Why?"

"Because I want to spend time with you. May I?"

"I thought you were spending this last day before surgery with Mateo."

Tension bristles through him at the reminder of his procedure tomorrow. After weeks of appointments and tests, we've come to this: the procedure. Rico's esophageal echocardiogram revealed an ASD about nine millimeters in diameter. Tomorrow, Dr. Thomas will plug that hole. And I will be there, waiting and worrying with his mom.

Rico responds, "Mamá took him out to buy a pair of swim trunks that fit better, and then they're getting lunch. Which means I have a couple hours to kill and a few ideas on how to kill them."

"Oh, do you now? You're nothing but trouble when you get ideas, Rico Rodriguez. However, I already agreed to join the guys at The Rusty Bucket for Darts & Drafts after work."

"Wrap it up, Dee," Watts hollers. "We need to head back to the station for shift change."

I nod to Watts and turn back to Rico. "You can come if you want to."

"Oh, I want to come," Rico says with a smug grin.

Stepping closer so I'm in his space, I challenge him. "But darts ain't no spectator sport, Rico Suave. If you want to come, you have to play."

I wink at him, then turn and jog past Pamela and Leroy with a wave before I climb up into the driver's seat of the engine.

"How's Romeo?" Drew asks over the headset radios as we go back to the station.

I roll my eyes again—I've been doing that a lot lately—and say, "You know Romeo and Juliet died at the end, right? That's not a love story—it's a tragedy. You need to work on your references. Maybe go with Westley and Princess Buttercup or Princess Leia and Han Solo."

"Pretty sure you'd break both my arms if I called you Princess," Drew responds, and the guys all laugh.

He has a valid point.

Sunlight slashes across the scuffed wooden floors of The Rusty Bucket as someone swings the door open and walks in. Everyone in our back corner of the bar turns to see who's entered the building, but I'm the only one who keeps staring as Rico walks across the room to join us back here.

He's so sexy. The slight limp on his left side from the residual numbness of the stroke is almost imperceptible. I perceive it, of course, because it's my job to recognize injuries, but to the layman's eyes, Rico is just a hunky Adonis with a bright white smile. Not that there's any "just" about it.

"Hey," Rico says as he comes to me.

The guys pretend to ignore us, but they see all. They're perceivers like me.

I contemplate my next move. Rico and I have spent a lot of time together lately. If I'm not accompanying him to appointments or meeting him for meals when our schedules align, we're sneaking around to get in some frisky alone-time action.

But we haven't said much—to each other or the rest of the town— about our relationship. It's like old times, back when our easy childhood friendship just naturally evolved into more as we grew up. These days, though, with all our baggage, I want to be careful, more deliberate in my decisions and actions when it comes to Rico. But the fucker is irresistible, and all I want to do is spend every waking minute with him.

It's a problem. That Rico-magic magnetism coupled with the worrisome hole in his heart have colluded to push aside a few key conversations. Like: Who are we to each other? What are we doing here? What does our future look like? He keeps calling it love, but what does that even mean to him these days? What does it mean to me?

Case in point: Rico comes to stand in front of me and turns that bright smile on with a wink. All those teenage-horndog pheromones whoosh through me, and instantly I forget about the conversations we haven't had yet. With one wink, he makes me stupidly smitten, and all I want to do is kiss him.

So I do.

It's not a big tongue-y kiss, just a peck. And I only wrap one arm around his neck when I reel him in and plant my lips on his. But it's enough to make this thing of ours official, sealed with a public kiss.

But in a town like Krause, everyone knows it's more than just a kiss. Everyone hears the silent promises I've made to him—and I hope, trust, he's making those promises to me too—right here in front of my crewmates and my dad and all his barfly buddies. With this kiss, I'm claiming Rico…officially…again.

When I pull away, Rico looks dumbstruck. He knows what it means too. His grin goes wide. I just shrug.

"Hey, man." Drew claps Rico on the shoulder, and they do some elaborate handshake and hug maneuver; male affection is so complicated. "Good to see you up and at 'em! How are you feeling? Dee says the procedure is tomorrow."

"Yep." Rico nods to Drew. "Feeling all right, thanks to you and Dee. I owe you a beer for that quick save."

Drew chuckles. "Well, I definitely won't turn one down."

Once the greetings and introductions are out of the way, we start a game of 501 darts with Drew, Rooster, Watts, and our buddy Kramer from Engine 12.

Rico plays poorly on the first few sets, which isn't a surprise. While he's getting by well since the stroke, his dexterity took a hit. His aim with his left hand is off; darts bounce off the wire more often than they impale in the sisal fiber of the board.

Despite his obvious handicap, Rico is betting large on himself, challenging the guys to a friendly wager. Normally, we gamble for shots of whiskey, but considering Rico has a heart procedure scheduled for tomorrow morning, no one is encouraging him to drink. So the bet is a $50 pot to the winner. I put my money in the pot, too, even though I know it's a sucker bet.

Sure enough, when it's Rico's turn to throw, he switches hands. And there it is, the reason you should never bet against Rico.

"Hey now," Rooster crows, "What's this? Are you...what's it called...?"

"Amphibious," Drew offers.

"Ambivalent," Watts suggests.

"Hardy har har." Rooster rolls his eyes at the guys, then shouts, "Oh! Ambidextrous!"

Rico shrugs, then he hits a triple twenty, a triple eighteen, and a double sixteen. He turns around with a wickedly bashful grin.

"You dirty dog!" Rooster hoots.

"Dart shark!" Drew agrees.

Rico looks over at me and waggles his brow. *Oh, it's on now! Challenge accepted!*

When it's my turn, I step up to the line, sway a little on my feet to loosen up, and then I throw one, two, three in quick succession: two triple twenties and a double eighteen.

I howl and fist-bump everyone on my way over to my beer and Rico.

He stands back, watching me with heat in his eyes. He leans close. "Think you can beat me, baby?"

The flirty tone of his voice, the warmth of his breath, the challenge in his words; they all do tingly things to my nervous system. "Oh, I know I can."

The guys laugh and drink, barely putting any effort or arithmetic into their games, but when it's time for Rico or me to throw, it's all quiet as they watch us do what we do best: compete.

"How about a friendly wager just between us?" Rico asks in a whisper, his breath hot on my cheek.

"What did you have in mind?"

"Whoever wins this round gets to pick the position."

I roll my eyes. "Oh really? You're assuming we'll be fucking later, eh?"

"Of course we'll be fucking later!" he says, loud enough I'm pretty sure my crew heard. Hell, my dad probably heard from all the way up by the bar.

And I'm not inclined to argue, so I take the bet. "If I win, I'm on top. I want to pin you down and ride you like a bucking bronco."

A slow grin spreads across Rico's face. "I might be inclined to let you win."

"You better not, or I'll ride you right to the edge and stop."

"Ouch. Okay." He considers for a long moment, then leans in a little closer. He's so far into my space that he's all I can see, all I can feel, all I can smell, and when he speaks, he's all I can hear as his deep voice teases. "If I win, I want you face down and ass up, your hands braced against the headboard while I fuck you so hard you come screaming my name."

Well. Shit. Now I'm the one inclined to let *him* win.

With a soft kiss to my cheek he asks, "Deal?"

"Deal," I manage to say as I take a sip of my iced tea to cool myself off.

"Yo, Rico, it's your turn, man," Rooster hollers.

Rico walks over to the line and throws another strong round. So do I. And back and forth we go, aiming to get to 501 first as the other guys enjoy the show.

Finally, when we're both on the finish, I go for it. Stepping to the line, I consider my options. I need 124 points. After doing some quick math in my head, I decide on a triple nineteen, a triple seventeen, and double eight. With a deep breath in and out, I throw.

It's a hit, a hit, and a miss…

What the fuck?

I frown at the board where my third dart sticks askew from the double sixteen, giving me sixteen more points than I need to check out. It's a bust.

How did I miss that? I look up at the air-conditioning vents, wondering if a strong breeze knocked my dart off course.

"Tough break." Rico pulls the darts out of the board, looking cock-sure and very annoying as he adds in a whisper, "Start stretching those fine legs, baby. I have a few more positions in mind, and I sure don't want you to hurt yourself when I tell you to bend over and grab your ankles."

If looks could kill, Rico would be resting in pieces right now. But they can't, so I step away from the line to watch him flawlessly throw a triple twenty, a triple eighteen, and a double twelve to check out.

Fuck.

All around me, the guys celebrate Rico's victory. He pockets the cash and coaxes me away from my fixation on the air-conditioning conspiracy, looping an arm around my waist and pulling me up against him. "I'm ready for my real prize, baby. You gonna give me what I want?"

I don't need anything more than those words to shift my focus away from losing the set and onto Rico, the winner. With a grin, he has me fixated on his mouth, and I'm practically begging for him to take his prize. "Let's go."

After I pull into my parking spot at the apartment in my precious purple Priscilla, my favorite black Charger rolls into the space beside me. We walk up the stairs together in silence. I know better than to distract him with kissing and flirting when we're on the stairs. He has a firm grip on the railing as he makes sure the slight drag of his left foot doesn't trip him up.

But once we're on the landing, all bets are off, and some of our clothes are on their way off too. I hustle to unlock the door, and before I've even pulled the key from the knob, he's on me, hands groping, mouth tasting. I giggle, and he growls, grabbing my hair and pulling my head back so he can nibble my neck as he asks, "Something funny?"

I really like it when he gets feral like this. And I like to get bratty and poke the beast. "*You're* funny. Growling like a caveman, so desperate for me."

"I'll show you a fucking caveman," he says as he bends and picks me up, tossing me over his shoulder and carrying me toward the bedroom. We leave the door hanging open, my keys still in the lock, and I don't care. I don't care about anything when Rico gets like this.

Since his stroke, since we reconnected, it's like he's out to prove something. He fucks me wholeheartedly, like there is no defect, like there was no stroke. Our sex is aerobic and exhausting. I love it, and I think he needs it, to prove to himself he's still strong.

He tosses me on the bed and gets on top of me, pressing my whole body into the mattress, his hard cock grinding against my backside. "You know what I want, baby. Push that sweet ass up and give me what I won."

God, yes. I moan and press my palms to the headboard as I rub my ass against his cock, begging him to make good on his promises from before.

To my great excitement he does, yanking at the button and zipper of my pants to get them down my thighs, and then his palm cups my head and pushes my face into the mattress as he works his own jeans. I turn my head enough to be able to breathe, and I cry out from the agony and ecstasy as he shoves his cock deep inside me.

"That's my dirty girl." His breath burns my cheek as his voice growls in my ear, and his weight crushes me into the bed as he takes me so fully, fucking me completely as he wraps me in his entire body, his arms around my neck, his legs pinning mine, his hips pistoning mercilessly against me. "You like it when I take you rough, don't you, baby?"

"Yes, God, yes." The words come out in little huffs of breath as he rams home over and over, and I can hardly breathe, and it's so hot I'm going to explode any second.

But then he comes to a full stop, and I cry out, desperate for more. He unwraps his arms from my neck and balances on his knees behind me, slowly sliding his cock in and out as his hands clutch my ass, groping roughly. This works too. I mewl and writhe beneath him, then yelp when he spanks me.

Left hand to left ass cheek. Right hand to right ass cheek. He does it over and over again. I cry out from the sharp sting of each slap and groan from the deep burn they leave. It hurts so good. Rico has gotten kinky with age and experience, and I love it. Being with him now is such a strange combination of old and new, familiar and unknown, and apparently, it's exactly what I need from him. As much as I have always and will always love the Rico I used to know, I'm extremely fond of this newer version of him too.

When my ass is pretty much lit on fire, his weight comes back on top of me, crushing me into the bed as he starts to fuck me hard and fast again. "That's for tomorrow. When you're sitting in my hospital room beside mamá, I want you to feel that burn and think of me, remember what I do to you, and how much you fucking love it."

Jesus, I'm going to come right now, just from the dirty talk. With his weight all over me, crushing me as he's fucking me, he shoves his free hand between my thighs and presses against my clit, rubbing me just right, and I come in an instant. The orgasm quakes and spasms through my body, sending me bucking beneath him as he keeps fucking me, keeps touching me, drawing it out, bringing me to orgasm again and still again in a whole chain reaction.

And then he comes, too, shaking on my back and bellowing at my ear. Covering me, crushing me with his wonderful weight as he fills me with his come.

Fucking hell, I love this man.

"What time?" I sit on my sore ass at the table, watching Rico cook a late lunch at my stove.

He's in just his jeans, and I'm mesmerized by his back, his toned muscles shifting as he flips food in the skillet. I can see the shrapnel scars on his shoulder, and a few new purplish spots around his neck and shoulders, bruises already forming from our afternoon delight. When you fuck rough while on blood thinners, it leaves marks.

"Mamá is taking me to check in at seven, surgery is at nine. I'll probably be out of surgery by eleven, so you could turn up then."

What's this "you could turn up at eleven" nonsense? Who does he think he's talking to? "I'll be there at seven."

Rico quirks his lips into half a grin, like he half expected me to say that. He comes to the table and serves up some chicken and veggies. We eat together as the radio plays in the background. I like these times with Rico. The sex between us is amazing, but these quiet times we share are much more intimate. "What's Mateo going to be up to tomorrow while we're at the hospital?"

Rico smiles. "His tios are taking him to Volente Beach for a day of fun in the sun."

"That sounds perfect. Does he know the surgery is happening?"

"He knows I'll be having a 'procedure' at the hospital. We decided not to provide more detail than that. He's too young to understand it all, and he gets nervous when we talk about my heart condition. He's afraid he's going to lose me."

Oh God, my heart breaks for that little boy. His mom is out of the picture, and now this scare with his dad too? All the more, it makes me appreciate Rico's brothers coming to stay and surround Rico and Mateo with family while they go through this.

After a moment, Rico says, "I'm a little scared too."

"Rico, this procedure is minimally invasive, with an extremely low mortality rate. You're young and fit, you're a low risk for complications. By tomorrow night, you'll be back home with a mended heart and a long future for you and your son to spend together."

Rico grins as he finishes his food and wipes his hands clean, then reaches for one of my legs. Pulling my foot up onto his lap, he starts massaging. After a twenty-four-hour shift, nothing feels better than this. Not even all those screaming orgasms can top the full-body relief I get when he works his thumb along the ball of my foot. With a moan, I move my other foot onto his lap.

He gives me the funniest look, a combination of amusement and affection as he rubs both my feet. "Mamá keeps telling me to marry you."

"What?" I sit up so quickly my feet come out of Rico's grip and hit the floor with a pair of thuds. But seriously. *"What?"*

Who said anything about marriage? We only just announced we're a couple today with that kiss at The Rusty Bucket. And now he's casually talking about marriage?

Still talking about his mom, Rico says, "She's old-fashioned, believes that marriage should come before sex."

"We've been having sex since we were seventeen."

"She didn't know we were having sex back then."

"Oh, you naïve man." I stand and take our dishes to the sink, focused on scrubbing them clean. Trying not to think too much—or at all—about Rico's casual reference to marriage, like it's nothing. I realize that for someone who married because of an accidental pregnancy, maybe it *is* nothing. Just a legal status change. But for me, marriage means something.

I scrub those plates until the shine wears off, then shut off the water and take a deep breath before I turn to face him and give him a piece of my mind. "Okay, listen up because I'm only going to say this once. The man I someday choose to marry will sweep me off my *fucking* feet. He will make me feel adored and loved and understood and needed. He will *not* just casually mention *maybe* getting married someday because his mom is old-fashioned. He will *not* treat marrying me like it's meaningless. He will want to marry me because I am as essential to him as the air he breathes. And his proposal will be an event, a *spectacular* event. I will not settle for anything less."

"As well you shouldn't," Rico says. "You're the most incredible person I've ever known, and you shouldn't settle, ever, for anyone or anything."

"Glad we're in agreement."

He pushes his chair away from the table and pats his lap. "Come here."

I have half a mind to refuse. I'm still mad. But Rico's lap looks so inviting, and I love the things that happen when I go to him. I should let him apologize to me properly. So I straddle him on the chair and smirk when he presses his forehead to mine.

"I'm sorry," he says.

"For what?"

"For acting so casual with you. Everything is so…easy with you, being with you just feels natural, you know? But that's no excuse for me taking you for granted. I need you like I need my heart to beat, but sometimes I take it all for granted. And for that, I'm sorry."

He angles his head and kisses me so gently, so sweetly. It's a heartbreaking kiss, I know, because it's broken me for any other man. This kiss cements all my feelings, making it abundantly clear to me that, despite how infuriating he is, I love this man.

When he slowly pulls away and presses his forehead to mine again, I open my eyes and stare deep into his. It's like drowning, being so totally adrift in all these emotions, treading water as I hang onto him for dear life.

Then he devastates me further when he kisses my forehead and whispers, "If I survive tomorrow, I will sweep you off your feet, baby. I will convince you to love me again. And then I will convince you to marry me. I want it all with you, and I will do anything and everything to win your heart back."

I blink away the sudden rush of tears and swallow the lump in my throat as I clutch his cheeks between my palms. "*When* you survive tomorrow, not *if*."

Today is the day. And I'm terrified.

They keep you awake for the event. And I just want to know: Who in their right mind would want to be awake during heart surgery?

Dee keeps reminding me that it's not "heart surgery"; it's a "minimally invasive heart *procedure*." But that's semantics. People are going to poke around in my heart, and all I get is this little valium to calm my nerves. I swallow the valium and give the nurse my friendliest fake grin as she turns to leave.

It's just me and Dee in here for a moment. Mamá went down to the cafeteria to collect a pair of coffees for them. None for me. Maybe that's why I'm extra irritable today—it's not the impending heart *procedure*, it's the lack of caffeine.

Turning to Dee, I flop my hospital gown aside as I complain, "They manscaped me."

Dee blinks at me then looks down and giggles. "Oh my God, it's so cute! Like a little mohawk for your dick."

I grumble more.

"Stop your bitching, Stroke Boy. The dick mohawk is for your own good. They have to access your heart through one of the veins in your groin, and you don't want some stray pubic hair getting into your heart, do you? So boom, dick mohawk."

Dee's logic is sound, and gross, and it makes me even more cranky. I've never been one of those guys who shaves it all. I *trim*, sure, but now my cock has a mohawk. A cockhawk, if you will. I flop my hospital gown back down. And it's just in time because mamá comes back into my room with two steaming cups of mouthwatering coffee. This is cruelty.

I turn my attention to the television, some documentary about the Texas Killing Fields playing, and after a few minutes, I don't care about the documentary, or the coffee, or my cockhawk. The valium must be working.

When the time comes for my procedure, I'm ready. For the first time in weeks, the flutter in my stomach isn't nerves, it's excitement. For myself, my son, my family, and my love, I want to be mended.

When the nurses come for me, mamá smothers me in hugs and whispers a prayer. Then Dee leans down and gives me a sweet, lingering kiss that makes me want to stay a little while longer. But they roll me away, out the door, and down the hall.

They push me into the operating room, and it's like I've been wheeled onto the bridge of the USS Enterprise. The technology here is out of this world.

I'm rolled to the center of the room, beneath a massive lattice of tracks used for moving lights, monitors, and machinery to where they're needed. A handful of helpful aides shift me from my patient bed to the operating table. Someone covers me with a paper cloth that adheres to my skin around the incision site, providing a modicum of privacy for me and my cockhawk.

Overhead, an X-ray machine is arranged directly over my chest. To my left, a monitor as wide as a movie screen displays the black-and-white X-ray image of my beating heart. And at my right, my doctor and his assistant stand behind a plexiglass screen wearing X-ray aprons with turtleneck collars, affording them maximum protection from chin to shin.

My doctor informs me we're beginning, and I nod as a pinch of pain hits at the top of my thigh. Almost as soon as I feel the injection of anesthesia, I feel nothing but the sensation of pressure at the spot where my leg meets my abdomen. I'd rather not think about all that, so I turn my attention to the television, watching my heart beat.

After my stroke, my editor cut me some slack on the number of hours he expected me to work, understanding I'd need more rest as I recovered. The one condition was he wanted me to write a piece about my experience.

Taking the assignment to heart—so to speak—I've recorded all my experiences from the night of the stroke to everything that's happened since. I've researched heart conditions and stroke statistics. I've conducted hours of interviews with medical professionals, including the team who saved me the night Dee and Drew rushed me to the ER. And now? I observe it all.

I'd told my editor I would be awake for the procedure. He insisted that was absurd, but here I am, awake and watching it all on that big monitor. It's weirdly fascinating to see this sterile, black-and-white view of my heart, my circulatory system; all that blood is invisible from this perspective.

The catheter my doctor inserted into my right femoral vein moves on the monitor, wiggling like a worm up toward the right atrium of my heart, and I can't feel it. It's like I'm observing someone else's ASD closure on the screen. There on the massive monitor, in bloodless black and white, the catheter reaches the hole inside my heart, and the doctor works to plug it.

At my side, the doctor and his assistant calculate the size of my heart hole, deciding on an eleven-millimeter plug, which someone retrieves from a cabinet in the corner of the room. Then they fish that up into my heart too.

I can't tear my gaze away as things start to happen on the screen. I hardly blink and definitely don't move a muscle as one end of the device expands in my heart. It looks like an umbrella, opening up to cover one side of my heart hole. A few moments later, a second part of the device expands within the second chamber of my heart, holding the plug in place between these two caps.

There it is—my shiny new ASD closure device. It looks like a flying saucer hovering in the cosmos of my chest, space alien technology right inside my body. It's so…

"Cool," I say as I stare, mesmerized.

The doctor replies, "It is pretty cool, isn't it?"

"Can I get a copy of that image?" I ask.

"Sure," he says as he instructs one of his aides to grab a few still images for me.

Once that's done, focus turns away from the device in my chest to the incision in my femoral vein. Because, despite my bloodless view of the procedure, there is quite a lot of blood coursing through my veins. The doctors move quickly to remove the catheter and seal the delicate incision in the vein. I remain silent and still, not wanting to distract the doctors as they ensure I don't bleed to death.

When my incision is stitched closed, the room fills with people and activity. The X-ray machine is shut off and moved, the monitor slid back into its resting place. The doctors shuck their X-ray protection and leave with friendly farewells.

Someone hands me a couple of pills to take, explaining they will prevent blood clots from attaching to the device. But I'm not allowed to sit up or move in any way. I can't swallow pills lying down, so I chew them and take a few sips of water through a straw to wash the chalky taste away.

Then, it's time to put me back on my waiting hospital bed. For that task, two big, burly nurses come in and instruct me not to move a muscle as they shift me from table to bed. Someone pulls the paper sheet off me and replaces it with warm blankets that feel so freaking amazing.

I revel in that warmth as I'm moved out of the fancy operating room and back to my waiting family. The moment mamá and Dee see me—still alive—their pensive expressions turn soft with relief, and their reactions fill me with more warmth than the cozy blankets.

It feels good, to be loved, to be on the other side of the procedure, to be healed—

"Okay, now, you cannot move *at all* for the next four hours," my primary care nurse instructs me. "We want to make sure you don't pull your suture open at the incision site. So stay horizontal, don't bend your legs, don't move. If you need anything, use this call button. Do you need anything right now? A sip of water?"

"Uh." I blink at her. "Yeah. Water."

And thus begins the worst part of the entire procedure. I don't think the procedure itself took more than an hour, and now they want me to lie here, completely still for four times that long? Jesus, when did I get so restless? I'm like Matty when I tell him there's something he can't do, and suddenly, he's singularly focused on doing that precise thing.

Groundhog Day plays on television, which seems weirdly appropriate. The story of a man, stuck, with nothing but time and boredom. I can relate.

"What are you doing?" Dee asks, her voice shockingly loud after so much quiet. "Why are you moving?"

I glance down at myself and realize I've shifted my legs a little, like I'm going to bend my knees. "Oops. I...forgot."

"Oops. You forgot?" She looks angry at me. "You *forgot* that if you pull the suture in your femoral vein open you could bleed to death in under five minutes?"

"Uh...yeah?"

She smirks and raises a brow. "Don't forget again. You have two more hours to follow one simple rule, Stroke Boy. Now lie still."

Damn, she's sexy when she's bossy. I glance over at mamá, who silently watched this exchange with an ear-to-ear smile and wedding bells in her eyes. With a huff, I turn my attention back to the movie and remain very, very still.

Eventually, *finally*, I'm allowed to move, but not much. I'm granted permission to waddle to the bathroom in my hospital socks and a gown sporting a few blood stains, a reminder that I had a doctor poking around in my heart this morning. The nurse gives me a clean gown to change into before I take my first post-surgery piss. In my room, she changes out the blood-stained sheets on my bed.

Now, when I return to lie down for the second four hours of observation, I'm allowed to adjust the bed so I can sit up a bit. And, *finally*, I'm fed. Salisbury steak and canned peaches—it's a feast. They bring meals for mamá and Dee, too, and it's nice eating together. It's relaxing to have them both here.

Once I've eaten and am feeling friendlier, mamá calls Javi to check in, and I'm handed the phone so I can talk to Matty. "Hey, big guy, did you have fun with your tios today?"

"I did!" Matty's excitement bursts through the phone line. "I got to swim all day and ride on the waterslides *four times*, and I had ice cream for lunch, and there was a pirate ship with a rope bridge and…" I close my eyes and listen to my son beam about his wonderful day. All my irritation and exhaustion melt away.

"That's awesome, Matty."

"And I ate broccoli at dinner because Tio Javi said I could stay up late to wait for you to come home but only if I ate broccoli so…" He finally takes a breath before asking, "When are you coming home?"

I grin from ear to ear. "I will be home by eight. You think you can stay up that late?"

"Uh huh! I will!"

"Then I will see you soon."

"Okay. I love you, Daddy."

"I love you, too, Matty."

When Matty hangs up, I stare at the phone for a moment before handing it to mamá. She smiles though she looks a little teary. I glance over at Dee, who looks like she has something in her eye too.

With *Addam's Family Values* muted on the television, it's silent for a moment before Dee says, "You're a good dad, Rico."

What do I say to such an incredible compliment? Mostly, I think I need to argue. I feel like a mediocre father, passable at best, but definitely *not* good. "Matty makes it easy."

"And the fact that you won't take credit for your job as a father is just one more thing to love about you."

My jaw drops, and I blink at her, struck dumb. Did she…? Wait. Hang on. Did she just admit she loves me?

CHAPTER 23
DEE

Shit!

I think I just admitted my feelings to Rico.

His jaw drops, confirming my fears. Yep. He heard it.

I just casually said the big L word. It's out there now, filling the air between us. And with Inez here as a witness, I can't gracefully walk it back. But in all honesty, would I want to?

From the chair in the corner of the room, Inez quietly stands and slips her purse onto her shoulder. Thankful for a reason to look away from Rico's intense gaze, I watch her collecting the items she brought with her this morning.

"Don't mind me," she says in a bright, chipper voice as she packs up her books and blanket. "In fact, why don't I head on over to the house? I can help the boys tidy up and get everything ready for you. Dee, I trust you'll bring him home once they clear him to leave?"

"I… Uh… Okay."

Within a matter of seconds, Inez kisses her son on the cheek and scurries out the door, leaving me alone with Rico.

"What just happened?" I ask him.

Rico gives me a devilish grin. "Mamá heard what she wanted to hear."

"Which is what, exactly?" I sound defensive because I am feeling defensive and stubborn and cornered.

"That you love me, *exactly*."

"I didn't say that. I said there are things about you that I love. There's a difference."

"Well, I love all the things about you, Deidre Marie Fletcher." He winks when he adds, "wholeheartedly."

"Smooth, Rico Suave."

The nurse comes into the room—just in time to interrupt some of the intensity of our conversation—and checks Rico's bandage. She applies pressure to his wound, confirming his incision site is still intact. Rico yelps in pain. I think he's about to complain, but the door opens again and in walks the cardiologist.

"How are we doing?" he asks.

Rico, still grimacing from the nurse's checks, grumbles, "Ready to get out of here."

"Well, everything looks good, so we're ready to get you out of here too. You'll need to keep your wound clean and unbandaged tonight so it can breathe a little as it heals. If you take a shower tonight or tomorrow, don't scrub the incision site. And no squatting or lifting anything heavier than ten pounds for the next seven days. I've written you a prescription for the blood thinners. Get that filled tomorrow and start taking those daily. You'll be on them for three months. I want to see you back here at that point for a checkup. Oh, also," he reaches into the packet of Rico's discharge papers and pulls out a couple pages, "here are the images you requested."

Rico stares at them, so I look, too, staring over his shoulder at an X-ray image of the device in his heart.

"Wow," I say.

"Right?" Rico agrees.

"It's so neat!" I bend to look a little closer. I can make out the shape of his spine, which helps orient me on the location and size of the flying-saucer device that's plugged the hole in Rico's heart. How interesting.

Once the doctor leaves, the nurse returns to sign Rico out, giving him even more paperwork. I collect his clothing from a bag in the cabinet by his bathroom and help him dress in the loose-fitting sweatpants and T-shirt he wore when we checked him in earlier today.

Rico is like a kid on Christmas morning, so excited to be leaving and returning to his family, able to finally relax, healed and whole. I manage to keep him walking at a gingerly pace as we head outside. I run ahead and bring my car around, then circle the hood so I can help him get in and strap his belt on.

"Those images are really neat," I say as I drive through the dark—at some point during all that sitting and waiting, the sun set on us—and nod at the images of the ASD device Rico holds in his hands.

"Yeah, pretty wild, right? I'm not sure if the quality of the images will be good enough though."

"Good enough for what?"

"For my article about the stroke."

"You're writing an article about the stroke?"

He harrumphs in agreement as he thumbs through the packet of papers the nurses sent home with him.

"When did you get so interested in journalism?"

"In Afghanistan, I used writing as therapy. I wrote about the experiences that hurt me the most and started submitting them as articles to the *Army Times*. It became a fairly popular column, like it was therapy for my readers too. Managed to get a few pieces into *Stars and Stripes* as well.

"When I got stateside, I knew I wanted to write. So I got a job at a weekly in San Antonio and took a lot of coursework at the community college toward a degree. When I moved here and went into Dan's office with some of my clips, he hired me on the spot."

"It sounds like you're happy here, with work, the town." I'm a bit embarrassed by the comment, like it shines a bright light on my insecurities, my long-held fear of abandonment, and specifically abandonment *by him*.

I glance over, and I'm struck by how genuinely joyous his expression is. He's truly smiling, and in that moment, he's the old Rico I remember. "I am. I love my job. I love this community. I love being close to my family and you. And Matty is happier here than I've ever seen him. I think back to when I left to join the Army, and I can't remember why I did it. Everything I need"—he rests his palm on my thigh, and I revel in the warmth of his touch—"every*one* I've ever needed is right here."

I don't dare look at him. My focus on the road, and I offer a generic greeting-card response. "Sometimes you have to leave to come home." Right on cue, I turn into Inez's drive and announce, "We're here," in a ridiculously loud and chipper tone. Once I've put us in park, I shut things down and hustle around the hood to help Rico out. He walks well enough on his own, but I still hover like a helicopter mom.

Inez swings the door wide before we can try the knob. I open my mouth to say my goodnights and take my leave, but she holds a finger to her lips, then whispers, "Welcome home, mijo, how do you feel?"

"Sore, stiff, why are we whispering?" Rico asks as he steps through the door, and he reaches for me, lacing our fingers together, pulling me inside.

I go with him. Of course, I go with him.

"Mateo tried to stay up, but he's exhausted. He's asleep on the couch. They all are."

We come into the main room to find Rico's two brothers draped awkwardly on the couch where they fell asleep watching television. And between them, Mateo is curled into a ball, with his head on a throw pillow and an afghan covering him.

It's adorable. Clearly, their day of fun in the sun wore them all out.

Like he can sense he's being watched, Manny Junior wakes suddenly with a snort and blinks his eyes open, getting his bearings. When he sees Rico, he leaps off the couch and comes at him with his arms out, a big bear of a brother looking for hugs.

"Gentle," I caution with as much assertiveness in my voice as whispering will allow. "He's just had surgery."

"You called it a procedure before, but *now* it's surgery?" Rico chides me with a smirk.

Manny remains frozen, his arms wide, his eyes bouncing between us.

Rico waves him over. "It's only my groin you have to be careful about."

"Trust me, hermanito, I'm not going anywhere near your groin," he says with a chuckle as he wraps his baby brother in a sweet hug.

The commotion wakes Javi, who comes to greet us too. First, they connect with Rico, whispering sweet brotherly love as they hug him, and then they come for me.

They act like I'm family too—they always have. Coming from a dysfunctional family, I always loved being part of Rico's, and it's like nothing has changed. Like to them, I'll always be one of them. While that might be standard operating procedure for the Rodriguez family, for me, these hugs have meaning, so much meaning.

Once we've run the gauntlet of affection, Rico goes over to the couch and sits beside his sleeping son. He reaches for Mateo, like he's going to lift him up. I hate that I have to stop him. "You can't lift anything over ten pounds right now, baby. Straining could reopen your wound."

The look in his eyes breaks my heart. All he wants to do is pick up his sleeping son and hold him. And I'm the killjoy who's in the way. I come around the couch and help Rico lift the pillow under Mateo's head so he can slide in close. This kid is a heavy sleeper, hardly stirring from all that commotion.

Rico strokes his palm over his son's back and then brushes a few strands of hair out of his face as he softly speaks, "Matty, I'm home."

While the commotion didn't stir him, his father's voice does. Mateo slowly wakes, blinking his eyes open, and he springs up, clambering to climb his dad for a hug. He's all elbows and knees, and I'm glad that throw pillow is on Rico's lap to protect his incision site.

After nearly choking his father with affection, Mateo settles onto Rico's lap and tells his dad all about his amazing day, again. Rico smiles wide as he listens, and it's the second time I've seen him smile like that since his return to town, since the stroke and all the madness surrounding it, since his surgery today fixed the biggest problem that's plagued Rico lately.

Weirdly, the sight of his joy triggers tears in me. It's the most beautiful thing I've ever seen Rico do, and it's yet another reason I forgive him for everything that happened between us.

These emotions are confusing and strange. I don't understand any of what I'm feeling right now. It's probably just exhaustion. I turn to quietly take my leave and let the Rodriguez family enjoy their time together, but I find Inez there, blocking my path to the door.

In a hushed voice, so as not to interrupt the precious moment taking place on her couch, Inez explains, "The boys and I discussed it earlier. Mateo can sleep in my bed tonight, and Javi will switch rooms and sleep in Rico's old bed so you two will have some extra room."

Wait. What?

Probably sensing my shock, she adds gently, "Of course, Dee Marie, you don't have to stay the night if you'd rather not. I certainly do not want to make you feel uncomfortable or obliged. But honestly, no one can keep that boy in line like you can. It would be helpful to have you here, reminding him to take care of himself."

Damn. This is weird. Is Rico's mom matchmaking right now? She's literally setting us up to sleep together. But he's just had surgery…on his groin. It's not like this is a mom-sanctioned sexcapade.

Of course, I have EMT training. I know how to properly and efficiently apply pressure to stop a massive bleed. It's smart, really, to keep me around. That's what this is.

So I nod and accept her invite, awkwardly. "I… Uh… Okay…"

Inez disappears down the hall. Rico turns to me, sharing a perplexed look and a chuckle. But seriously: *What just happened?*

Once Mateo has finished updating his dad on his adventurous day, he starts to drift back toward sleep again. I can tell how much Rico wants to carry his son to bed, but Javi volunteers, and so they get Mateo down in his abuela's bed for the night, and Inez turns in too. After some grown-up conversation between the brothers about today's procedure, we all start yawning, and it's time for us to get some sleep.

No one says anything about me staying over. They all just act like it's the most natural thing in the world for me to be here, spending the night with their baby brother. I act like it's natural, too, even though this is the first time we'll fall asleep together at night and wake up together in the morning.

I try not to think about that as Rico strips his T-shirt off, and I help with his pants. I pretend not to notice how close my face is to his gorgeous cock. I keep things professional when removing the bandage over his incision to let it "breathe," as the doctor ordered, making sure it's still healthy and intact.

As hot as he is when he's naked, none of this is about sex. It's about caring, and that makes it more difficult to keep my head on straight. Sex is easy. It's transactional. Caring—it's hard and messy and meaningful.

I turn away, giving him a pat on the arm to let him know he can lie down. Then I get ready, pulling my bra off through the sleeves of my tee and kicking off my sneakers and jeans before I join him in bed.

But I can't sleep. I'm wired, twitchy, and full of questions. This is absurd. How am I supposed to relax when I'm in bed with the love of my life, he's totally naked, and his mom and son are asleep on the other side of the wall? *Ugh!*

Giving voice to one of my concerns, I whisper, "This is strange. What if Mateo gets the wrong idea?"

"What's the wrong idea?"

I don't know the answer to that question. What are we? If Matty sees us together, assumes we're together, is there anything wrong with that?

"Look, I understand your concern, and I appreciate it. But even if you decide you don't want to be with me romantically, I hope we will remain as close as we always used to be. You've been my best friend since I was eight … No, more than that. You've been part of this family. You still *are* part of this family. Matty adores you, I adore you, my whole family adores you as one of our own. You have as much right to be here as anyone."

"Sharing a bed with you?"

Rico loops an arm around me and squeezes me tighter against his side. "That's just bonus."

"This is all very confusing."

"Confusing good or confusing bad?"

"Isn't all confusion bad?"

"I don't think so. Sometimes confusion is filled with hope. My current state of confusion, for example, is chock full of hope."

"What is it you hope for, Rico?"

"I hope for everything, with you."

Well… Shit… I'm sinking deeper and deeper into all these *feelings*. Like quicksand, the more I struggle, the more I sink.

So I stop struggling. I cuddle a little closer to him, letting myself enjoy the comfort of his embrace. Rico plants a soft kiss on my forehead, and he inhales, like he's breathing me in. I've seen him do that with Mateo, and now, with me too?

That's what does it. That's when the emotional quicksand swallows me up. That's the moment when I let myself fall completely and totally in love with him again and let myself be loved by him again. And that's when I start to cry.

Like I once advised Mateo, I put all my old hurt feelings into the tears, and I let them out, all over Rico's chest. I sob as quietly as I can, and Rico hugs me, so tight, so strong, so protective. Like I'm safe with him because he understands how precious this thing we have is.

When we were young, we loved each other, but we took that love for granted. Now, we understand that life is precious, time is precious, and love is precious. I'm precious to him; I can feel it in his arms as they hold me, his lips as they kiss the top of my head. And he is precious to me too. He always has been. And he always will be.

I shift up onto my elbow and wipe my tears away as I look at him in the pale light of the moon. And I admit it, giving power to my emotions when I say, "I love you, Rico."

"Oh God." He pulls me so close I'm crushed against his chest as he kisses my head. When I look up, he kisses my mouth as he whispers such sweet words against my lips. "I love you too, baby." He finishes it all with a hand against my cheek. "Thank you."

"For what?"

"For giving me a second chance."

EPILOGUE
RICO

"Where are we going?" Matty asks with a definite whine in his voice.

I grin and shake my head. "You'll see. Have you cleaned your bedroom?"

He nods in that way that tells me he's fibbing.

"If I go in there, I'm not going to step on any toys, am I?"

Matty considers, then runs off to his room, like he has more cleaning to do. I grin at the sight of him disappearing into his very own bedroom.

We've spent the last few weeks helping Drew, Chloe, and their cats move out of this place and into their dream house on the other side of mamá. Then Matty and I moved in here.

The house is perfect for him, perfect for us. It's a great place for a kid to grow up, especially with his abuela living right next door. Plus, there's the massive deck outside, perfect for watching the sun rise. The first thing I did was build him a swing set, too, so he's got a space to run and play with friends. Though we're still working on helping him find friends in his class. Today's little adventure might help a bit with that.

I'm finishing up the dishes and drying my hands when the front door swings open, and Dee comes in, fresh off her shift, looking so damn hot in her uniform pants and station T-shirt. She glances around, sees we're alone, and jogs over to me for a quick make-out session in the kitchen. She pretty much climbs me like a tree, her legs wrapped around my waist, her ass perched on the counter as I kiss the hell out of her.

Her shifts are too long. Twenty-four hours apart is *rough*. I can't get enough of her, ever. I'm ready for her to move in here, to make things official, but Dee deserves romance, so we're taking our time, dating when our schedules align, and longing for each other when they don't.

"Dee!" Matty squeals when he sees who I'm ravaging in the kitchen.

Dee pushes off me and hops down from the counter to hug Matty and pick him up. He thinks he's too big for me to hold him, but he lets Dee. I'd be jealous if I didn't love it so much to see him take to her like he has.

"Where are we going?" he asks her.

Dee glances at me, and I roll my eyes. Matty has no chill when it comes to surprises, which is why we're keeping this one a secret to the bitter end. A lesson in patience. Dee turns to Matty and explains, "I can't tell you that. It's a secret."

"You can whisper it to me."

"Whispering is still telling. If I tell you, I'll be violating your dad's trust. Do you know what that means?"

Matty sort of nods.

Dee adds, "When people tell me secrets, I want them to know they can trust me to keep those things secret. You know, if you ever want to tell me a secret, I want you to know that you can trust me to keep it, okay?"

We've been talking about this a lot lately. I've been taking Matty to therapy sessions for a couple months now, and the doctor suggests we encourage him to share his feelings, fears, and anxieties. So far, Matty doesn't seem interested in sharing, so I change the subject.

"Good news!" I announce as I tickle the bottoms of Matty's feet. "Now that Dee is here, we can go see your surprise. Are you ready?"

"Yes!" Matty squeals, grinning from ear to ear.

I tickle his feet again, delighted by the sound of his giggles. "No, you're not. Go get your shoes."

Dee sets Matty back on his feet, and when he races down the hall and into his bedroom, I yank Dee back against me and take another taste of her mouth. She's so sweet, the best kind of candy. I can't wait for tonight. She already agreed she'll sleep over.

After Matty is finally fully dressed, and we manage to get out the door and pile into my Charger, I make sure he's all buckled into his booster seat before we take off toward town, then keep going past it. The sat nav points us up and down hills, in and around curves as we weave deeper into the Hill Country until it announces we've reached our destination. I turn onto a long gravel driveway, which curves through the live oaks and mesquite trees, coming to an old farmhouse flanked by a pair of massive barns. Over the top is the sign, Cassie's Cat Castle.

"Daddy, it's a cat castle!" Matty announces with awe in his voice, and I love the sound of it.

"It sure is!"

"What's a cat castle?" Dee asks, right on cue.

"Well," I pause to put the car in park, then turn to Matty, "it's a place where some really nice people help scared little kitty cats feel safe, and then other nice people like us come and adopt a kitty cat."

Matty's eyes go huge. "Do I get to adopt a cat?"

"You do!" I love the smile on his face. I love that I put it there. Best surprise experience ever. "You get to pick any cat you want, and he or she will come home with us to live and play on the cat jungle gym, okay?" The house has felt too empty without Bodhi and Utah running all over the tracks that loop the walls. And I think a pet could be good for Matty as he settles into his new home and new life in Krause.

Matty has no chill and starts to wrestle with his seat belt. I spring into action and help him out of the back seat while Dee introduces herself to the petite older woman who's come out to greet us.

"Welcome to the Cat Castle! You must be Mateo," the woman, Cassie, says as she shakes my son's hand. "Well, head on into the barn, and see which kitty cat is your favorite."

Matty goes bouncing into the building, and Dee and I follow. We watch him as he runs around chasing cats and kittens. But he seems a little shy about petting any of them, so Dee and I approach, each of us squatting to his level and petting some of the chatty, purring cats who come looking for affection. Soon, Matty is doing the same, really connecting with a pair of black and orange kittens.

When he's is clearly comfortable, chasing the kittens as they roll and run and frolic, I clasp Dee's hand, and she squeezes as we smile, enjoying Matty's joy.

"Beautiful family you have," Cassie says.

"Couldn't agree more." I loop an arm over Dee's shoulders.

"Looks like Mateo likes PB & J."

"PB & J?"

"The kittens. They're a pair of tortie females from a recent litter. The one with green eyes and a lot of orange on her face is PB, while the one with blue eyes and mostly black patterns on her face is J. They're nine weeks old, fully vaccinated, and ready for their forever home. But they come as a pair."

"A pair?"

Cassie maintains her patience with me as I keep repeating what she's saying. "Yes, you mentioned on your adoption application that you were looking for one indoor cat. But PB & J are inseparable and very sassy. They would not approve of separation, so neither shall we."

Dee giggles, and I smile ear to ear as we cross through the cat paradise to hang out with Matty and his two favorite cats, PB & J. Within the hour, we've decided they're the cats for us.

Cassie sets us up with a cat carrier and some other essentials to get them home, and soon we're all crouched around the travel crate in the center of the living room, the food bowls and litter box set up where they now belong, ready to introduce the kittens to their forever family in their forever home.

It takes them a few hours to grow comfortable with us in this new space and relax. No one's purring by bedtime, but I know it's only a matter of time before they are as at home here as the rest of us.

Tucking Matty in for the night, I'm a little sad when he doesn't ask for a story, but the big grin on his face as his new cats curl up around him puts my smile firmly back in place. This is what Matty needs right now. He knows he will always have his dad, but he needs friends, too, and PB & J are going to be the best sleepover buddies this sweet little boy could ever have.

I arrange his door just right, with the hall light on, then head to my bedroom. Inside, I find the woman of my dreams, my best friend and true love, lying naked on my bed, reading the newspaper.

Out loud, she reads, "I survived a war, only to come home and nearly die in my mother's house of a broken heart. But my heart was mended. From the doctors with their space-age technology to my family with love and laughter, I was made whole again." Then she closes the paper and looks up at me. "Damn, baby, you're a hell of a writer."

Part of me feels an "aw, shucks" response coming on, but the other part of me can't take my eyes off her naked breasts as she rolls onto her back and grins at me upside down, like she's offering herself up on a platter. She's a feast I won't refuse. Stripping in a hurry as I cross to the bed, I lie beside her, taking one of her nipples into my mouth as I pinch the other between my fingers.

I'm still on the blood thinners, so I've learned to be a bit gentler than my usual balls-to-the-wall style, but I've come to really enjoy this, the slow, methodical way we worship each other as we make love. It's like learning a new side of each other, of ourselves.

As I slide inside her, and she arches above me, I wrap my arms around her and pull her down against my chest as I move slow and deep, reveling at the sweet sounds she makes. This is heaven, this little life of mine. I'd taken it for granted all those years ago, and then I'd torn it apart on that awful night in Afghanistan.

The doctors would probably argue with my science on this, but I firmly believe that was the night I ripped a hole in my heart. A birth defect, nah. It was trying to live my life without Dee in it. But finally, my heart is mended. I have my love, the missing part of my heart, right here in my arms. And I'll never grow tired of telling her, "I love you Dee, with all my heart."

She gives me that gorgeous, sex-drunk smile of hers, and responds, "I love you too, Rico, whole-heartedly."

EXTENDED EPILOGUE
ROOSTER

The look on Dee's face when Rico's Charger comes to a screeching halt at the curb of the firehouse is priceless. She turns away from scrubbing the hood of Engine 31 to see what's going on. I glance over at Drew, who waggles his brows at me.

It's go time!

Rico gets out of his car and waggles his brows at us too.

Hell yes! This is going to be fun!

Watts must hear the commotion from his office inside because he comes out as well, ready for the show.

"What's going on?" Dee asks Rico, but her question is cut short when the passenger door pops open and out comes Chloe, looking terrified. *Shit.* Rico was supposed to tell her it wasn't anything to fear. Chloe is a worrier, God bless her sweet soul.

"Is everything okay? Rico said you needed to see me." Chloe hurries across the lawn as Drew hops down from the hood of the engine—leaving the soap suds to spot. She practically tackles him, and it's so damn cute the way he soothes her fears with nothing more than a big warm hug and a soft kiss.

I can't help but grin at the sight. I've known Drew for a while now, and I've never seen him happier than when he's with Chloe. It's so sweet, it's going to give me a cavity.

"Seriously, what the fuck is going on here?" Ah, Dee, our precious little porcupine, comes to the rescue with a toothpick to keep these pearly whites cavity free.

Rico is a brave man, not withering an inch under the scrutiny of her scowl. His big smile seems to curb her annoyance enough to soften her posture as he hugs her without answering.

Little do they know that it's me who holds the answer to their questions. Literally, I'm holding the speaker.

It's been weeks of covert practice sessions, where I played the role of Bob Fosse, whipping these love-struck boys into shape for their big production, and all I get to do is press play on the music. Which I do as soon as I get the thumbs-up from them both.

Beyonce's "Single Ladies" starts up, and instantly Rico and Drew sync into the choreography we've been practicing all those nights the ladies thought we were having Guys Night Out. I'm impressed—the boys can dance when they want to, and today, they want to.

"Oh my God. What is happening right now?" Dee asks Chloe as they stand together, their jaws agape in shock as their men bump and grind and shimmy. It's so… Well, it's pretty hot. A few of the neighbors and dog walkers stop to watch too.

"It's like our own personal *Magic Mike* show," Chloe remarks.

"No. Better," Dee says. "It's like *Magic Mike XXL.*"

"Oh, yeah, totally. Good call." Chloe nods in agreement.

As the chorus starts up again, Dee asks loudly, "Put a ring on what? Cuz the way y'all are gyrating is giving me ideas."

"Girl, same," Chloe says with an adorable laugh.

The chorus reaches the bridge and transitions to a new refrain, and that's when the guys work in the spin we finally nailed this week, managing to each end up on one knee, side by side in front of Chloe and Dee.

These single ladies must be a little slow because it's only then that the penny drops. Or is it pennies drop, since it's two pennies…? I'm getting distracted. Point is, the moment the guys plant their knees on the ground, Dee and Chloe figure out what this whole production is about, and the looks on their faces are priceless. I zoom the video in on this perfect moment: my other job for the day's event is documentarian.

"Wait… What's happening right now—OH MY GOD. Is this?" Dee asks Rico.

"Why are you on your knee? Oh my lord, what are you doing?" Chloe asks Drew.

I turn the volume down on Beyonce so the boys can be heard and zoom in further as Drew pulls a box out of his pocket. He pops it open to reveal a sparkly ring. He's been storing that thing here at the station for weeks, waiting for this big day.

Chloe gasps and giggles as she starts to tear up and cry. "I half expected it to be a cat collar."

Hmm. Kinky.

Drew chuckles. "You already wear my collar, baby. Now I want you to wear my ring. I've loved you since the moment I laid eyes on you… Okay, after that first weird fight, but since then I've wanted to spend every waking moment with you and the sleeping moments too. I've never felt this close to anyone…ever…and I want it all, forever. I want a family and I want it with you. Will you have me? Will you be my wife?"

Now Chloe is full-on crying, heaving silent sobs. It's a weirdly beautiful and heartbreaking moment, and it makes me a bit jealous that I've never known the feeling she's experiencing right now. Love looks intense and kind of awesome, but I wouldn't know.

Drew tugs her a little closer so she sits on his propped knee. With the hand that's not holding the ring, he wipes her tears away and kisses the tip of her nose. After a moment, she wipes her tears away, too, and lets out a little giggle that is just the cutest thing.

Drew stares at her expectantly, finally asking, "Do you have an answer for me?"

"Oh, shit, yeah, I mean yes. Definitely yes. Totally yes."

With that, Drew slips the ring on her finger as she stares at it in awe, like she's confused. Then he collapses his knee out from under her, and they both fall to the ground in an adorably cuddlesome heap, laughing and kissing and smiling like lovesick fools. *Sigh.*

I shift the camera to the other couple, where Dee's mouth gapes in shock as she looks at the ring Rico is holding up as an offering.

"I can't take that," Dee says.

I blink, stunned. Oh shit. Is she turning him down—?

"Dee, you can—"

"You just said that's the ring your father gave to your mother. I can't—"

"You *can*! Mamá wants you to have it, my brothers want you to have it. If he could speak from the grave, I'll bet you a hundred dollars my father would want you to have it."

Dee just frowns at him.

Sensing that he's losing her focus, he starts talking fast. "Deidre Marie Fletcher, this ring comes from my family, and if you accept my proposal, it will stay with my family because you are my family. You always have been.

"From the time we were eight I've belonged to you, Dee, in mind, body, and soul. I let myself drift away from that truth for too long, but now that I'm back, and I see what life can be like when I'm with you, it's all I want, always and forever. You were my first. You'll be my last. You're my always, Deidre Marie Fletcher. Please, baby, marry me. Let me be your first and last and always too."

Okay, I'm crying a little now. Between the gentle way Drew is making out with Chloe and the soft expression on Dee's face as tears roll down her cheeks, I'm a mess. I try to sniff quietly as I adjust the camera to capture the look of absolute astonished happiness on Dee's face.

She shouts, "Yes!" and tackles Rico in a hug, kissing all over his face as he tries to wrestle that heirloom ring onto her finger.

I pan out to capture both happy couples as they seem to melt into each other, completely oblivious to the world outside their little love bubbles. They don't even notice when the neighborhood dog walkers cheer and hoot. I cheer too. So does Watts. It's a happy day when not one, but *two* members of our crew find their happily-ever-after person. I glance over at Watts, who grins knowingly from ear to ear. Like the two couples making out on the lawn, he knows what love is. He's blissfully in love with his wife and their precious daughter. I'm the only lonely heart here. The odd one out, not that that's anything new.

"Well, there you have it," I say when I turn the camera on myself. "Two weddings to attend, and here's me without a date." With a sigh and a wink at the camera, I stop recording and post it to my social channels. When that's done, I jump off the hood of the engine and join everyone down on the ground for hugs and smiles and a look at the rings. The couples are so happy, and their joy is contagious.

There's a reason so many one-night stands start at weddings. Nuptials are an aphrodisiac. Perhaps it's for the best that I don't have a date. Leaves me with options. Maybe I'll meet Mr. Right in the coat closet of someone's winter wedding.

Keep reading for a glimpse of **Hearts We Claim**. Leashes tangle and sparks fly when Rooster is out walking a foster dog and runs into the town's new veterinarian Markus.

HEARTS WE CLAIM

CHAPTER ONE - ADAM

The sun beats down on the shoulders of my dress blues, baking me like a potato wrapped in foil. God, it's hot out here. And that's saying a lot, considering it's my day job to walk through fire.

But it's not the weather that's the problem, it's the formality. These pristine white gloves, the neat rows of brass buttons down the front of my jacket, the crisply ironed pleats of my pants, and the regal Pershing cap on my head have me sweating.

I'm a casual guy. Most of the time, my job lets me relax in cargo pants and a FIRE T-shirt. But today, I've had to haul my dress blues out of deep storage to stand here, looking stoic and professional for the ceremony.

Rows of plastic folding chairs dot the neat lawn in front of the gazebo bandstand, which sits in the center of the park between Krause's historic library and city hall. Friends, family, and neighbors fill the seats. Peeking out from beneath the shadowy brims of cowboy hats, moving the air with hand fans, they watch our pomp and circumstance with community pride. And there is a good reason to be proud. Today is a big day for the Krause Fire Department.

My compatriots and I stand in two perfectly neat lines beside the bandstand, while up on the platform, Fire Chief "Big Mac" McKenna announces his successor: Watts. Well, he's Chief Watson now, but he'll always be Watts to us. When Big Mac caved to the pressure from his wife to finally retire, there was no doubt who he and the city would name as the next chief.

Watts has worked in fire service for twenty years, he's earned this promotion, and he's the first person of color to hold the top job. It's big news in this small town. Dee's fiancé, Rico, is here to report the story for the local paper, and I stand extra tall for the photos. Watts is making history today, and it couldn't be more well deserved.

With a plaque, a solid handshake, and a hearty back pat, the job passes from Big Mac to Watts, and the community erupts in applause. Drew, Dee, and I join the rest of the fire department with loud whoops and hollers in celebration.

Once the event is behind us, and we've posed for photos and

mingled with the attendees for a while, I pocket my gloves and tuck my Pershing cap under my arm as I find my fire crew and their families in the shade of a nearby oak tree. Watts's wife beams at her husband as she asks if we're coming over to their house for the pool party.

We all answer in some form of the affirmative as we watch Mateo and Aaliyah, Rico's son and Watts's daughter, play chase on the wide green lawn. When we split up and walk toward our vehicles, I'm already stripping out of my clothes. I've slipped off my jacket and tugged my tie loose before I've even made it to my truck. Once I get there and pop the door open, I strip out of the rest. Toeing my patent leather shoes off and slipping out of my socks, too, I stand barefoot in the street and pull off my pants. I'd worn a pair of swim trunks rather than boxer briefs under my uniform for precisely this reason: rapid costume change.

I slide my feet into an old pair of sneakers, toss my fancy dress clothes onto the passenger seat, and pull myself up on the running board to get into the driver's seat. But when I reach for the door to pull it shut, I pause.

I'm being watched. Frowning just a little, I turn to stare at a guy who stands at the corner of Main and Vine. At his feet sits a well-behaved, large-breed dog—a pit bull lab mix, if I had to guess.

I grin at the dog, then look up and hold the man's gaze, grinning a little at him too. He's just watched me strip mostly naked. And, even after I've caught him staring, he doesn't look away. His brilliant blue eyes—which I can see in surprising detail, even from across the street —practically gleam with humor and…is that curiosity? A small smirk stretches across the man's handsome face, and I'm mesmerized.

Who is this guy? Krause is a small town, and you can be damn sure I know everyone here, especially a seriously fine man like this. I'm certain I've never laid eyes on him. I'd have remembered that mouth and the dark tousled hair. And those eyes—Jesus those eyes are like sapphires sparkling in the sunlight.

He keeps staring. And I keep staring back at him. Clearly, he's curious, and so am I. But the connection between us is severed when he looks down at his phone and turns to answer it. Disappointment sinks into my chest, but I don't let it linger.

Today is a beautiful day, and I'm late for a party. With a shrug, I shut the door, crank the engine, and head west to Watts's place.

I drive with the windows down, enjoying the refreshing breeze. It's a hot day for mid-October, but that's never bothered me. I'm a Texas boy through and through; I can handle a little heat.

Watts lives in the newer part of town, where, fifteen years back a small development of acreages replaced an old ranch. Folks around here still call this area the "old Koenig farm" instead of its fifteen-year-old name, "Pleasant Valley Estates." But things move slowly here, and everything that's happened since the turn of the twenty-first century, was "just yesterday."

Cars dot the driveway and the road around me, and I recognize most of them. All my crew mates and their partners are here, as well as a lot of folks from other shifts at Station 31 and other stations around the county.

I walk around to the back of the house, letting myself through the gate and heading toward the chatter of revelers and the squeal of children. Watts's backyard is lovely, the reason they bought the house. Wide and private, it's ringed by spindly oaks and mesquite trees, and at its center, the crystalline water of a swimming pool glimmers in the sun.

As an adult, I know I should head over to where the grownups have gathered around the grill and cocktail table to chitchat. But my inner child can't pull his attention from the sparkling water or pass up the opportunity to make an unforgettable entrance to the party.

From a good fifty feet away, I take off at a sprint across the lawn. At the last moment, I leap into the air, pull one knee to my chest, and, with a Braveheart battle cry, execute a perfect cannonball, coming down with a massive splash.

When I pop back up, I'm greeted by the sounds of applause and excited squeals from the kids dog-paddling around me in the pool. I give everyone a big dumb grin and announce, "Let the party begin!"

Several adults point out that the party already started without me, but the kids are delighted by my entrance. Mateo and Aaliyah and their friends swim around me, asking how they can do cannonballs as big as mine. I use the opportunity to impart some wisdom. "You've gotta grow big and strong like me," I flex a bicep to demonstrate, "so eat all your vegetables. Got it?"

The kids crinkle their noses at the thought of vegetables and chatter among themselves, comparing the strength of their little arms. I swim to the ladder to hoist myself out, only just now realizing I forgot to take off my shoes before diving in. Thank the baby Jesus I left my phone and wallet in the truck.

As for my sneakers, they've been through worse. I kick them off and leave them in the sun to dry. Shaking the water out of my curly hair like a shaggy dog, I wiggle my fingers in my ears to unclog them. Drew has pulled a beer from the cooler and offers it my way, so I walk to him and gladly accept. We clink bottles as I take my place among the adults.

"Girl, you should see him. I was like, 'you can check my pussy anytime,' " Chloe says to Dee with a laugh shared between them, and Drew, Rico, and I all turn to stare, wide-eyed.

"What?" Drew asks for everyone, but mostly for himself and his sole claim on Chloe's pussy.

"The new vet. I took Bodhi and Utah for their shots on Thursday, remember?"

"Yeah, and what does that have to do with checking *your* pussy?"

Chloe laughs and throws her arms around Drew's neck, teasing as she says, "Bodhi is your pussy, and Utah is mine, and when we get married, they'll be our pussies."

Drew smiles wide. He does that every time she talks about the wedding and marriage. I never would have pegged Drew for a romantic, but he's such a smitten kitten when it comes to Chloe.

Then Chloe tacks on, "Also, the new veterinarian in town is sexy as hell. I invited him to our wedding, so you'll get to meet him soon."

Drew's smile sinks into a frown, and Chloe giggles as she kisses his sour puss away.

Rico glances over to Dee. "Have you invited him to our wedding too?"

"Not yet, but I will. Gives me another excuse to watch him play with our pussies."

Rico laughs, and the two happy couples get cuddly with their canoodling. It's been a few months since Drew and Chloe and Rico and Dee got engaged in a dual dancing proposal, which I helped choreograph, and I could not be happier for them. But, sometimes it's difficult being the odd man out. Forever the single guy, the gay guy, the sidekick, and friend.

I wander to where Watts is explaining the best way to grill burgers.

"You want your meat juicy, don't you?" Watts sounds like a drill sergeant as he breathes down the dude's neck. "So don't press them too hard."

"Nothing better than juicy meat," I quip as I approach and give the guy a proper once-over as he cooks the hamburger patties to Watts's exacting specifications. He looks to be in his early twenties, slightly taller than my six-foot-two frame, and built like he lifts a lot of weights. He's handsome without being pretty and flashes a drop-dead gorgeous dimple in his cheek when he looks up and smiles at me.

Watts sees me, too, and raises his beer to clink against mine as I join them. "Rooster, meet Knox County. He's your new crewmate."

"Knox *County*?" I ask, amused by the name.

"Rooster?" Knox counters.

Fair point. I run my fingers over my damp red hair, and he nods, understanding. People have been calling me Rooster since I was born with a head of red curls. My hair isn't carrot-colored these days, more of a deep burnt-umber shade, and I keep my tight curls cut into a wide, low-maintenance mohawk so it doesn't slow me down when donning my bunker gear. Still, it's never difficult for people to understand where the nickname comes from.

"Welcome," I say to Knox, and we clink bottles. I could ask him more about his own name, but I'll save it for our next shift. "Guess I'll be seeing you at the station tomorrow."

With another nod, we all turn our attention to the grill and talk about the weather. No shop talk for now; there will be plenty of time for that when he's learning the ropes on the job.

CHAPTER TWO - ADAM

"Good girl! You're doing so well," I coo at Drusilla.

She glances over her shoulder to give me a goofy grin—her left ear flopping with her strides as she matches my pace—then turns her attention back to the road as she runs beside me, careful not to get ahead and pull the leash. I'm impressed.

Mom's newest rescue is a Shepherd and Rottweiler mix who was removed from a hoarder with dozens of neglected and malnourished dogs in his yard. Drusilla was just a puppy, barely weaned, when she came to Mom's shelter, and already she'd suffered far too much. She had worms, fleas, and part of her tail was missing, probably bitten off by an older dog in the horde.

In the month and a half since Mom took her in, she's grown by leaps and bounds. Her coat has come in thick and lustrous, and she has tons of energy, always wiggling and wagging that nubby little tail. She's adorable and a very sweet girl with a chill disposition that makes her my favorite jogging companion.

At Main Street, we wait for the light to turn green. I run in place, while Drusilla follows my command to sit, looking dainty and desperate for a treat. Tossing her the liver morsel she's earned, I laugh when she swallows it whole. "Try savoring those treats every once in a while, Pretty Girl."

Drusilla yawns at me in response. When the light changes, and I stride forward, her excitement gets the better of her, and she darts ahead, tugging a little. I give a little tug back, reminding her who's controlling the pace. She takes the hint and slows to be at my side.

We jog past the courthouse and library, the two oldest and prettiest buildings in town. I take a deep breath of the mild morning air. Fall comes late to Texas, so any decrease in the temperature is greatly welcome.

The refreshing weather gives me a smile, and everything seems right with the world. But, when I turn at the corner to loop around the courthouse and head back home, it all goes horribly wrong.

Drusilla spots another dog coming our way, and in that instant she forgets all her training and darts forward to greet the other animal. I'm caught off guard as she tangles us in the other dog's leash and runs me right into the other dog's dad.

We collide hard, two objects in motion that have suddenly stopped. Jolted and irritated, I cuss up a storm. Of course, I don't cuss at the dog —she's young and learning. I'm the one to blame for not paying better attention, for not holding the leash more firmly. Then I look up and cuss for an entirely different reason.

"Fuck," I mutter as I catch sight of the person I've run into. Those eyes. That smirking grin. That tousled dark hair. It's him, the guy from the award ceremony, the one who watched me strip half naked.

Damn. He's handsome. Up close now, I can really see his eyes, such a luscious blue. And his hair—dark curls that wave in the breeze. My heart stutters in my chest, and I say it again, "Fuck… I mean… Sorry."

He chuckles as we manage to disentangle, and God that feels like a loss. His body felt so warm and solid against mine, and now there's just air, crisp fall air devoid of the heat I was enjoying only moments ago.

"Looks like they've made friends," the stranger says and directs my attention to the dogs. They're sniffing each other all over and whining with excitement. An instant connection for them. Puppy love at first sight.

I look back at the man standing so close. Good God, he's beautiful, and he just keeps smiling at me. *Instant connection.*

"I'm Markus." He offers his hand to shake.

I take it. Of course I take it; I will take anything this man gives me.

"Rooster," I say back.

"Rooster?" His brow furrows, and damn, even that looks good on him.

I smirk and use my free hand to gesture at my hair, stroking my fingers over the mohawk of auburn curls. "Like the red comb on a rooster's head."

"Ah, gotcha."

Do you though? Do you got me? I'm definitely game.

For some reason, I just start talking, telling him more about myself than he needs to know. "My real name is Adam, but everyone calls me Rooster—they have since I was born. I think it's a combination of the red hair and the fact I woke my parents up screeching to the sun in the wee hours of the morning."

Markus laughs, a lot. God, that laugh. It rumbles through me like thunder and pours over me like rain.

I try to think of more funny things to say, but I'm lost for words. And all at once I realize we're still shaking hands and standing awkwardly close together. Markus notices, too, retracting his hand and taking a step back.

With a commanding voice, he says, "Rufus, heel."

My body reacts to his strong tone. My mouth waters, and shivers run down my spine as my cock nearly stands at attention. I've never had a thing for dominant men, but right now, I'm definitely feeling the exception to that rule.

Markus's dog responds well too. The gorgeous pit bull mix pulls away from Drusilla and sits beside Markus. Drusilla is far less behaved when I try the same command on her, but eventually she sits with a whine.

"Rufus, good name," I say to fill the silence.

Markus smiles in response and nods to the dog at the end of my leash. "And this is?"

"Drusilla."

He furrows his brow and asks, "As in Caligula's sister?"

"Uh…" Caligula's sister? Interesting. Hot and smart. Check and check! "No, my mom is just a big *Buffy the Vampire Slayer* fan."

"Your mom named your dog?"

Okay, this conversation has gone sideways. I try to right it with another wordy monologue. "Drusilla is not my dog. She's a rescue. My mom runs a dog shelter and boarding facility on the north side of town. When I jog, I like to take a dog or two with me, to give them a chance to stretch their legs and socialize." I glance down at Drusilla, who has shifted onto her back so she can lick her genitals while she looks over at Rufus. *Uh…* Shaking my head in amusement, I look back at Markus and change the subject. "So what about you? Are you named after Marcus Aurelius?"

Markus lets out another deep, rumbly laugh. The sound does funny things to my nervous system, and my cock.

"No." His laugh turns a little wispy, like there's no air behind it. "My parents named me Mark after the Gospel of Mark, but I like Markus better."

Interesting. Everything about this guy is interesting.

Seeming anxious to change the subject, he turns his attention to Drusilla and gives her a toothless grin as he asks, "May I pet her?"

"Absolutely. She has a wonderful temperament."

Markus crouches to scratch Drusilla behind the ears, both the one that stands tall and the one that flops over a little. She whines with puppy exuberance, her stubby tail swishing a small patch of the pavement clean as she works hard to keep her butt on the ground despite all the excitement.

"You're a good girl, aren't you, Drusilla?" Marcus coos, and she's clearly smitten.

Drusilla tries to lick his mouth, but he expertly dodges her tongue as he smiles up at me. Jesus, he's sexy when he's down on his knees, doling out praise, those blue eyes staring up at me,—

Markus straightens to his full height. I'm relieved and a little disappointed at the same time. He's a hair taller than me, and our eyes lock as we both smile, silent for a moment, just staring.

This is a new experience for me—to be so attracted to someone here in Krause. I'm well known as the only gay man in this very small town, at least the only *outwardly* gay man. When I'm in the mood to hook up, I drive an hour out of town to San Antonio or Austin just to flirt like this.

I like it, this notion of a local crush, and I want to explore it. I'm about to ask if Markus wants to get a coffee sometime, maybe jog together; I could give him a tour of the town. But he interrupts my thoughts when he clears his throat and says, "Well, I best be off. I need to open the clinic at nine."

"Clinic?"

Markus nods and pats his pooch on the head. "Main Street Vet

Clinic. We just opened last week."

Of course! Markus is the new veterinarian who has all the local pussies purring. That conversation at Watts's promotion party makes much more sense now.

"Good to know," I tell him. "When Doc Evans retired and shut down the vet clinic, my mom had to take her dogs to Dripping Springs for shots and neutering. She fosters dogs, so it will be wonderful to have a local vet again."

"Great," Markus says, but he doesn't move to leave.

Neither do I. "Great," I mimic, and we both nod.

"Well," Markus breaks our eye contact, looking down at Rufus and giving his head a little pet as he says, "Let's go." Then to me, he adds, "It was nice to meet you, Adam."

Adam. He called me Adam. I melt from the inside out at the sound of my name on his lips. No one ever calls me by my name. It feels strange and special. Like, with him, I'm a whole different person.

"It was nice meeting you too, Markus. I'm sure we'll cross paths again."

"Looking forward to it," he says to me, then clucks his tongue at his dog. Rufus springs to his feet, and the two of them jog away, around the corner and out of sight.

Drusilla and I watch them go, then Drusilla makes a little whining sound that I feel in the depths of my soul. "Same, girl. Same."

Grab a copy of **Hearts We Claim** to keep reading
Adam, Markus, Drusilla, and Rufus's story.

While jogging with Drusilla, the awkward puppy drags me right into a tangle of leashes with another pooch and his person.

For the dogs, it's puppy love at first sight. For us humans, well, I'm certainly not complaining when I get a look at who she's tangled me with.

Tall, dark, and handsome: this must be Markus, the town's new veterinarian.

More than one gossiping granny has suggested he'd be perfect for me. Pump the breaks, Gladys, we don't even know if Krause's new resident is gay.

Though the dazzling smile he just gave me sure holds a lot of promise.

Hearts We Claim is a sexy, full-length, small town, male/male dog dads romance. Featuring a sexy firefighter hero and the town's new veterinarian, this is Book Three of the Hearts of Texas series, but it can be read as a standalone.

THANK YOU

Thank you for reading *Hearts to Mend*. If you enjoyed the story of Dee, Rico & Mateo, please spread the word!

xoxo,
Christina

And don't forget to subscribe to my newsletter
subscribepage.io/Td7TPB
or join my reader's group
facebook.com/groups/christinaswildberries
for the latest news and new releases.

ACKNOWLEDGMENTS

First of all, thank you for reading Rico and Dee's story. Seriously, thank you!

This book is intensely personal to me, and it has a strange origin story. It all began on August 13, 2022, when I suffered an ischemic stroke caused by an undetected atrial septal defect. I didn't know what was happening, and (stupidly) I did *not* go to the hospital that night. Finally, three days later, I went to the doctor about my "migraine from hell," and after an MRI, I was told the news. It took months of doctor's appointments, speech therapy sessions, and a space-age heart procedure for me to get back to some semblance of normalcy, but one side effect of the stroke lingered: I wasn't writing.

Well, that's not entirely true. I was writing plenty *about* the stroke. It was just the fiction writing that suffered neglect. And that's when I got the idea: put a stroke in your fiction, girl! And thus, *Hearts to Mend* was born. I had never intended for *Hearts on Fire* to be part of a series, but when it came time to throw a stroke into the mix, this story seemed like the best fit. Plus, I loved writing Inez so much the first time, I decided to bring one of her sons on board and give him a stroke.

Sorry, Rico. Thanks for being such a good sport about it.

Incredibly, this book did the trick with my stroke-induced writer's block, and I finished the final draft of it exactly one week before the one-year anniversary of the stroke. Not too shabby!

I could not have achieved this goal without a lot of help. And so, I say thank you, thank you, thank you to…

Dr. Thomas McMinn Jr., MD, and his team at Austin Heart Hospital for mending my heart. Liz Joiner, MA/SLP, LCSW at St. David's Rehabilitation Hospital, who helped me with my aphasia and my tendency to get "tangled up" when I was stressed or confused. Dr. Natalie A. Williams, MD, for realizing that the pain in my head was probably more than a migraine and ordered an MRI.

Big, huge, massive thanks to Meghan Scott for not only answering all my stroke questions while I was recovering but also helping me write the parts of stroke treatment that I missed because I didn't call 911 that night. You've been my number one fan since book one, and I hope you know I'm your number one fan too.

In addition to the help from my medical-subject-matter expert, this book required a lot of other subject-matter expertise, and I am so grateful to everyone who lent a hand in making this book the best it could be. Tom Madison, who has been a firefighting expert of both Hearts of Texas books, you rock. To Sean, Logan, Matt, and Jack, the guys of Shift B at Austin Fire Department Station 7, thanks for answering all my questions (even the dumb ones) and for the ride out on Engine 7. This book is so much better because of y'all!

Thank you to SGM (ret.) Jeremy Kagan and Libertie Smith for help with Army, deployment, and Afghanistan details. To my dad, Dave Berry, for your journalism and Army journalism help. To Lauren Cervantes and Enrique Flores for help with the Spanish language and Mexican American family details. To Brettany Boozer for answering my social work questions. To Paul McAniff, Yancy York, and Tom Groszko for schooling me in darts. And to my husband, Errek the Electrician, for explaining about ants and their fire-starter tendencies.

To my family and friends who were there for me every step of the way through the stroke, but also before the stroke and long after it: I'm lucky to have so many amazing, giving people in my life.

To Christina Consolino, probably the closest friend I have who I have yet to meet. Someday! You were incredibly supportive as I tried to edit the last book a week after the stroke, and you've been there the whole time through a trying year. I hope I've been as supportive to you. I call you my book bestie, even though that sounds so juvenile, but it's true. You are my book bestie!

To Erica Connor, you've been such an incredible friend and support this whole time, and now to have you on my team is freakin' amazing. I feel like I can touch the sky with your help. Thank you.

To every one of my readers: Writing keeps me sane, and sharing that writing makes me happy. Thank you so much for reading what I write! I hope you've enjoyed this one.

ABOUT THE AUTHOR

Christina Berry is an award-winning author of smart, smutty romance. A citizen of the Cherokee Nation, Christina is originally from Tulsa, Oklahoma, and currently resides in Austin, Texas. When not writing, she can be found helping her husband with their never-ending home remodeling adventure or spoiling their amazing dog.

WWW.CHRISTINABERRY.COM